RUMINATIONS

AUTHOR: DENTON DUSTON TAPLEY JR.

This book is dedicated to

Betty Tapley

Duston Tapley III

Jay Tapley

Linda Webber

who grudgingly put up with my nonsense

RUMINATIONS
(chew the cud one more time)

TABLE OF CONTENTS

A LA'MENT - ALZHEIMER'S

It took everything

You live with your wife for 60 years and all of a sudden the body you live with is there but the soul is gone, never to return or speak to you again but the eyes still look at you and she even smiles at you but never says your name or I love you, I miss you, where have you been? Are you coming for supper, have you talked to the children? What are they up to?

It's gone forever but the body is there constantly reminding you, I want to be with you, but cannot through no fault of my own or yours.

I am in there somewhere but can't get out, don't forget me or what once was.

Where ever myself is, am thinking of you and the children.

God knows I want to be there but something won't let me, I'm really trying, always believe that, really trying, but have been cursed by some unknown force that won't turn me loose, oh, help me, help me, God help me.

It is to no avail until circumstances have run their course and the husband will cry and the children will cry and the mother if there is a heaven is crying but they shall never meet again, what is gone is gone and will never return.

What can we do? There is nothing but to continue crying until the cup is full, dump, and cry some more, *ad infinitum,* until we all meet again, so the Christians and other Gods say, in a veiled place called heaven.

In the meantime shall live in a living hell without the wife and mother but the body form is still there where inside the mother is being tortured and the children and husband are being tortured outside. It is as if the purported Gods are against us. Where is some of that blood of Jesus that cures everything, send a flask this way to the wife, mother, husband, and children.

When is the missing loneliness worst? At night when all is quiet, thoughts creep into your head, what happened, where did everyone go? Did I hear her talk, laugh, or say hello, tell you to come to bed, or did you hear her whistle. She whistled well.

Something swells up inside of you, an empty feeling which you can do nothing about but it hurts and the tears come.

What is it that brings on the tears? Maybe because there is no end, a finality to this drama. She will be there screaming to get out unto eternity and the husband and children will suffer until their end. Who has played this trick?

Let the cold wind blow.

Let the cold wind blow.

FRED

God, I want to give you a situation and you tell me what you think. His name was Fred and I met him when we moved to Vidalia, Georgia in 1944. I remember we were in Mrs. McArthur's class and don't even know about how I would remember my teacher in the third grad in 1944 but I do, and Fred Tippett was in my class.

There are two things that happened during our school years which I particularly remember, well actually, three things I particularly remember. Back in 1944 there was no lunchroom at the Vidalia High or grammar school which was together then. Normally my mother would fix dinner for us and myself and my brother would walk home and eat and walk back to school and have what is called the afternoon school session.

At recess this particular day, Fred Tippet came up to me and told me he had forgotten his lunch and asked me could he go home and eat with me. Fred lived way out in the country and his aunt always brought him to school. I can't remember what I told Fred but it was that he couldn't go home and eat dinner with me although I knew my mother would not care but I didn't know what she was going to have for dinner and was worried it might not be good enough for Fred. I have never forgotten that and regret it and as it turned out on that particular day, my mother had fried my brother and I a little piece of cube steak and some vegetables which would have been a great meal. I could hardly eat for thinking about poor Fred back at the school with no lunch.

The second thing I could remember about Fred was that we were in the 9th grade which would have been probably about 1950 we still used desks where two people would sit at one desk. As it turned out, Fred was my partner at the double desk. We were just beginning to learn Algebra and I never will forget that no matter how hard I tried, I could not teach Fred how to solve a simple algebraic equation. The main thing I recall is that Fred never could possibly get his mind on 2x+4 what does x equal. He just simply had no interest in that concept.

We had a principal in school then called Carl Shealy and he and Fred and I were kinda talking friends and Fred was always telling us to come out and fish in the creek at his daddy's farm. One day Mr. Shealy and I went out and looked for Fred but he was gone somewhere so we went fishing in the creek anyway. We caught a couple of "red-eyes" but not enough to eat or anything like that. We decided to play a trick on Fred and not knowing and understanding things we took the fish and put them in the Tippett's mailbox. The next day Fred came to school and told us how upset he was and his whole family was that we would put those fish in their mailbox. I never really quite understood what the big deal was but it was not funny to them that they found fish in their mailbox.

The years went by and we all graduated from Vidalia High School in 1953 and sometime thereafter and I can't remember exactly, probably eight or ten years after graduation we decided to have a class reunion. Fred still lived in Toombs County but I was in the army for two years and then went to college and was not exactly a resident of Toombs County but still came home. I was married and he was married and I never really had much contact with him except at the reunion. I recall when he came in, we had our little banquet get together, Fred was on crutches.

The gossip that went around was that Fred had multiple sclerosis. And while he was not deathly sick the general consensus in these days were that multiple sclerosis was a progressing type thing and there was no cure. I remember the next reunion we had Fred came and one of his boys was pushing him and he was in a wheelchair.

Sometime way after that I had heard that Fred had gotten a divorce and remarried and gotten another divorce. I don't remember exactly but I received a call at my office and it was Fred. He was in the Meadows Regional Nursing Home and wanted me to come out to see him on some business he had. I went and Fred could not walk but he could still move his hands and do a little writing, turn his T.V. on and off, talk, and actually do most everything a person could do except he would not walk. He would occasionally get in his wheelchair. I noticed he lost the use of one arm, then the loss of the other arm and eventually could only move his head. When I first went to visit him he could answer the phone and turn his T.V. on and those kind of things but at the end he could not do any of those things and the only way he could answer the phone was to turn his head and bump a button which would answer the phone and he could talk.

Fred and I had some really good conversations all through those years, had a few laughs, talked about people, gossiped about this and that and just kinda sort of a pleasant visit. When I was there with him and believe he felt the same way, we sort of lost ourselves, he didn't think about his situation and I never thought about anything I had done that day or I was going to do in the future. The most striking thing about Fred was he never once whined or complained about his situation. When I first began to go around there I was amazed that he could laugh about anything or be cheerful about anything but he always was and never realized he was in the dumps about anything. Here was a person who laid there twenty-four hours a day and had only contact with whoever happened to walk in the room but he was still upbeat and cheerful. He still laughed and joked although he had little to laugh and joke about. The oddest thing of all, and this is what I want you to explain to me God, is I would go around there at 4:00 so down in the dumps, my head bloody and bowed and I felt like I was carrying a five hundred ton weight on my shoulders all as a result of working that week, dealing with aggravating lawyers and clients that even Jesus could not please, dreading to start again that next Monday and do the same thing all over. I was so unfeeling and unappreciative of my situation versus Fred Tippett.

It says something about the human spirit that they just cannot put themselves in the shoes of people that are less fortunate and stingingly can only think of themselves. I never felt sorry for Fred in a sense, but I thought about a lot of times what a great guy he was and for the things I should be thankful especially that I was not like Fred Tippett. I would go in that room with all these things running around in my head and sat there a few minutes and I would usually have to stand up so he could look at me and I could look down at him and after he would always ask me what was going on in good ole Vidalia and I would always give him the gossip and we would both get a laugh out of it. It didn't take but five minutes before I had forgotten all my troubles and it was sort of like we were in a room away from all the world and he and I were just talking and laughing, and joking. I was the one who benefitted from the visits and in fact was getting more than I was giving to Fred. I realized that after a while. Fred picked me up instead of me doing "my duty to visit". I believe Fred really appreciated me coming to see him but he didn't realize I was the person getting the benefit of the visit. The disease finally had its way with Fred. I will never forget those Friday afternoons we had together. I would just like to see Fred one more time and tell him how much I appreciated him letting me come and what he was doing for me and not what I was doing for him. I was the benefactor not the giver, although I tried.

WILLIE B REMEMBERS

Authors note: This narrative was written when it was announced in the Atlanta Constitution February 7, 2000 edition, that Willie B had died at the age of 41. Willie B. was a Low Land Gorilla born in Africa in 1958. He was brought to the Atlanta Zoo in 1961 and spent 20 years in a concrete cage with front bars to be viewed by the public. Author saw him and remembers his huge size and he had a tire on a chain and an old suitcase he threw around. It was a wondrous thing to see. Willie B was an icon. He was moved to green place from box (cage) where he had spent 20 years. He was moved to another cage where he could go out to green place. He was afraid and felt threatened (Friend keeper) stayed and slept in new cage with him until he would go out in the green place.

The author was moved to write this narrative in 2000 as if these were Willie B's thoughts and he was saying them.

I have this vague remembrance that comes and goes in patches, sort of like clouds passing over head where sometime the cloud is a remembrance, but then it passes and you only see the blue sky and cannot think anything about that.

I do remember a perhaps "warm feeling" without an actual picture in my mind of green bushes and fields and trees and a lot of others like me running around and being very close to someone and being held, snuggled and picked on the back, rubbed and feeling just wonderful. She was big and I was little, compared to her, and there were others small like me. We played. I can't even remember being hungry or cold or dissatisfied or really doing anything, like work or anything unpleasant, except scratching and raking and being around that other who was always nearby. I felt safe when she was there.

It was warm and green and comfortable. Then one day I remember there was a lot of excitement, loud noises, and strange others. I couldn't see the one that always looked after me anymore. I was in a box and couldn't see anyone and there were strange others around me and I remember being very frightened.

I thought of the one who looked after me a lot and had a sad unrequited feeling. I was fed and not hungry, sometimes cold and never really happy. I longed to run around and be back in the green place but was kept in this box.

Many others different from me would come and look and I would look back at them. I was very frightened at first, but then fright went away and a melancholy sadness replaced it.

As I stayed in this room, my recollection of the green place and the one who gave me comfort was less and less on my mind. My food was good and I became acquainted with another and looked forward to seeing him. He would talk to me and he would make noises to me. I would look at him and make noises to him and felt relatively good at times, but there was always that lingering feeling that something was missing and I could not become completely happy.

Long after my recollection of the green place, I didn't think of it very much but sat in my box and ate, and slept, and looked at those who came.

I sat there day after day in my box and it's like a fog that goes through my mind, but at times the fog clears just slightly although its murky and smoky, I see by remembering the green place and I travel there and like a dream am again holding onto her and feeling warm and this is stained in my mind for years and years as I sat in my box. I am not in the box any longer, but at the green place. Just remembering the green place gives me a sense of not being in the box any longer, to feel warm again. The bars are not as cold and confining, nor are the cement floors, because while I am here, I'm not there but I am in the green place.

Then one day it happened. I moved into a new place and looked out and saw a green place. Had the fog cleared? Had I been transformed back? What had happened? I smelled smells that I could only recall through the fog. I was happy my other friend was there with me when I saw the green place.

Would she be there? The one I felt so close to at the green place I saw through the fog. I could hardly remember her and my heart did not race because the view through the fog of the green place was not clear and I felt, more than remembering the other warm one. To touch the grass and see the green was something that even my aged numbness felt some solace.

I felt something warm on my face that brought back a veiled memory of the green place. I tried to touch but could not feel it. Was so satisfying. My feelings are numb after so long in the box but have a muted desire to stay in this new green place and feel the yellow light.

I have a numbed feeling for the others, but the others are all I have.

I remember holding onto her and feeling the warm light on myself for her. She scratched and picked at me, which felt very good. I felt a sense of good feeling to be in a new green place. When this invisible stuff blew on me and saw through the veil holding onto the other tighter when the invisible liquid would blow on us, I felt not afraid with her. I have long forgot how to feel afraid in this new green place.

I remember snuggling to her and nursing in the warm liquid it would fill my stomach and would feel warm, and satisfied, and in general felt good all over. It was a happy, good feeling all over. I have never felt that happy, good feeling since that time taken from her, put in a box, put in a larger box and the box became my whole place to be. I have never had that warm, happy feeling since that time and can hardly remember that warm, happy feeling.

They come and go and look at me and I look at them. Some laugh and talk, some don't say anything, and I just look and look and look. I look and look and look for seconds then minutes then hours then days then months then years then forever. After a while, I don't really see anything except they do come to feed me and I see the person who brings the food and even that becomes blurred. And then I can't remember except I have a yearning, which I can't remember what the yearning is for, or why I have the yearning, or exactly what I yearn for.

JOHNNY WIGGINS CAFÉ

It was about 1945 and we all went to one school, 1st through 11th (soon to be 12th) (kindergarten non-existent those days) to the school on the Mt. Vernon Hwy. My brothers and I walked (buses also were non-existent) to school about ½ mile every morning and back every afternoon and walked home for lunch and back to school for the afternoon session. On this particularly rare occasion my mother would not be home to fix lunch and gave me and my brother Jack fifty cents to eat at Johnny Wiggins Café located in Vidalia across from Shuman's grocery about where Church Street turned to McIntosh Street.

Mother gave us the fifty cents and instructions where to eat, Johnny's Café, which would be two hamburgers and two orange drinks a variable feast and an adventurous day on the town, to eat lunch during the week by ourselves (it was dinner in those days).

Carrying that kind of money was a heavy responsibility and felt it prudent to give it to my teacher to hold until dinner, get back at dinner hour and go eat at Johnny's.

On the dinner bell we took off, went to café and ordered two hamburgers and two orange drinks. We were proud. I was looking after younger brother, he was nine and I was ten.

All of the sudden I realized I had not gotten the money from teacher and we bolted for the door, made about three steps. Mr. Wiggins spied us and pointed his finger, said "where you boys going?" I said we forgot our money, he said (ordered us), to sit down and eat.

That was life in 1945 in Vidalia, Georgia, and was a time not ever to return, sad.

REMEMBER MOM

I wrote this to a colleague, an Assistant District Attorney, who when inquiring why she was absent from court, I was told her mother was terminally ill and she was taking care of her. Her mother passed and in a moment of sympathy to her plight wanted to assuage her pain and wrote this and my secretary delivered it in a sympathy card. She cried when she read it.

Remember when she held you, it felt so warm and safe, her arms would be around you not tight but right there and it was such a good feeling.

She would go away for an hour or two and remember how it was a thrill beyond description when she came back and you could not wait to touch her, and she smelled so good, that smell you will never forget and can remember now.

She would sometimes get on to you and even in those times you loved her and it was such fun to make up, soon forgotten, bathing was good times too, you felt so good after that.

She dressed you and no matter how you looked she made you feel cute, a special cute, and you felt it was true.

Sitting in her lap was comforting and loving, an ecstasy beyond belief, you were part of her and she was part of you.

Even in those hormonal teen years after a disagreement, it was like sitting in her lap again to let it pass.

The cord was never cut no matter how far away you were. It was good to know you could always go back to that lap.

As long as these memories are there she is always there.

PARIS FRANCE

I was 19 years old in the army and full of curiosity and wanting to see what the world's all about.

My friend and I decided to go to Paris, France on leave and he had a car so we took off.

We checked into a hotel and decided to go to the Moulin Rouge night life place, thought might run into Henri de Toulouse-Lautrec that is where the midget painter hung out and made Moulin Rouge famous.

We were walking down the street and every shyster in Paris recognized us as green as a gourd and could certainly be taken advantage of. We were flush with money, made $115.00 per month. It was crowded and we were walking and I made a somewhat flirty remark to this girl and her friend.

She was cute but her friend was strikingly good looking.

She immediately flirted back, isn't that what you do at 19 years old, fresh from Vidalia, Georgia, and knew everything. It's vague but believe I asked the girls to sit with us and have a drink, which they did. It was a happy time where the sap was rising and not a care in the world. The girl who had latched onto me, can't remember what happened to the good looking one but my friend was not too attractive and think she drifted away but we had agreed to go to the Rivera (that's French for Daytona Beach) the next day and were to pick up the girls the next morning.

On the way home my girl and I were in the back seat and remembering my training from Vidalia immediately attacked her. She resisted mightily and was stranded without even a good night kiss. Sorely disappointed.

When we picked up girls the next morning, the girl my friend was to take to beach did not show, her friend apologizing but my date did show.

We took off to the Daytona Beach of France, the Rivera, and immediately sought shelter, a place to stay. While I was worldly being from Vidalia, when we looked for an apartment my girl shopped for us, me not quiet understanding French , we don't have a Rivera in Vidalia. She immediately took over and made it plain this would be our suite and landlady pointed out we could move mattress out on to balcony and sleep out there. I pretended did this all the time, moving in with a girl at the beach and the balcony. In reality, I had never slept with a girl over night at the beach or anywhere else. I put on my suavest demeanor. I had just started shaving.

We stayed in our apartment and needless to say I thought had died and gone to heaven. We stayed three days and nocturnals and returned to Paris where she and I took a room together. My army leave was running out.

A knock on door and there was her extremely attractive friend and wanted to know if she could spend the night. We only had one bed. Later, the friend giggling kept asking why the bed was shaking. When the shaking stopped my girlfriend moved to foot of bed leaving Miss America and I alone at other end. While I am admittedly from South Georgia, I picked up on this pretty quick but shamefully did not want too and felt an allegiance for my girlfriend. It was a mistake I have kind of regretted to this day but even at nineteen there is a feeling of some loyalty and I cared for my girlfriend and did not want her to believe I had no feeling. The next morning left and never saw her again. She always said I would receive a box and in it would be a bambino, ours, but the box never arrived.

I stayed over past my leave but the army did not punish, I was a short timer. I have thought of this many times how good life is but it's just one of those shadows that flicks and flutters on the stage and is gone forever.

SHE NEVER MOVED

He liked girls and rather than get serious he would become their partner (he was married). They furnished him something and he furnished them something. Everybody was relatively happy. Girl partners fall into categories, some really enjoy it, some fake it and that's not too bad, some endure, and some really like and appreciate you as a friend.

Finding partners was a continuing chore as they would come and go, get married, get serious with someone, or maybe even go back to the husband. Not working was the answer.

Ask a friend, "know anyone looking for a partner?" I was directed to a bar maid he knew and she was extremely good looking, blonde, lithe, long legs, adequate bosom, friendly but a little straight forward, slightly business like.

The question is usually country-fide and slightly asinine forward like, "would you go out sometime and understand the partnership theory". She graciously declined and said was taken care of at that moment but would get back in touch if need arises. Don't call me, will call you.

She called several months later and partnership began. She was very beautiful and exciting, but relationship lacked a little something. It was sterile, methodical, trained, mechanical, very businesslike. You kept hoping she would spontaneous scream, moan, or excitingly ask, breathing heavily, how the weather was outside. With her everything went as planned, no interruptions, no one calling, no knocks on door. And then you began to notice and realize her pelvic area (for want of a better way to put) never moved the fifty or so times consummation took place. When say, never moved, no breeze blew, no chill bumps arose, all was quiet on the home front. Am convinced if an earthquake had occurred and floor with bed crashed from second floor to the ground, that pelvic part would not be disturbed or move.

It must be related to the psychic, philosophic mind, body, be true to yourself as well as to others.

It reminded of a story of the merchant seaman who came into port and fell in love with a woman who made wages by entertaining. It was not she was a woman of the night, prostitute, or very loose woman (whore). She did what she could to make ends meet, shoveling dirt out of the ditch and it didn't matter whose ditch it was or where dirt was piled and when she finished she never thought of ditch or dirt again or who paid her to shovel. It was what she did.

Then one night she had this funny feeling her hands became sweaty on shovel handle and actually began to care about the ditch digging and had a glow inside and felt the other was glowing. They married later and were together until his ship left to return later.

She had no money, so ditches were waiting to be dug for money. How could she be true and dig ditches, but had to eat. Reflecting, her thoughts of him were true, she would never give all to anyone but him and thereafter when digging ditches would never take her top off, she was being true, top off was only for him.

The partner above became a Registered Nurse (RN), married a member of a band and they had children. She contracted to travel for a company and would go all over the U.S., Company paid all expense, apartment, travel, per diem and when arrived husband would run an ad in the paper for music lessons.

When we were partners, she mentioned did I know an infertile couple where wife could not have children, she would have baby, surrogate mother, for them for $10,000 and might go to $5,000. There were no takers but several years later told me she had a baby that turned out to be babies (twins) for $25,000 for an Italian couple and because twins, thought fee should have been increased.

She saved pelvic movement for the person who made her hands sweat on the shovel handle.

THE HAIRLESS DOG

I'll never forget this little bulldog took up at our house. She was one of those little stub nose about 10 inches high. Have no idea from where she emanated. She was one of those little dogs that when you go to someone's house and there is a screen, he comes to door and jumps about 3 feet high up the screen with his ears sticking up and those eyes looking like they are bulged and may pop out any time. You worry about those eyes. All those dogs had ever seen was black.

This particular dog had no hair from neck back. The skin was black and he did not seem to be in any discomfort.

Another thing when we fed the dogs, can't remember what other dogs dominated our existence, but when we fed whatever he wanted to eat he grabbed and ran off a distance and hid away from other dogs to eat, probably a survival instinct. I thought this odd as our civilized dogs did not fight over food, they were a little too civilized some would call sorry.

He did this for a long time but eventually stopped and would eat where we fed. He would not in the beginning let you touch but later warily would let you briefly rub him.

He eventually became quite civilized, became a pet, and would hang around with us. He was a lovable fellow and always wondered where he came from and was obviously pretty close to pure bred. I believe he was abandoned because of his hair problem. The hair problem fascinated me, as it did not appear to be from a burn and assume it was a mange hair problem. He must have suffered greatly in the beginning of the disease.

I remembered my grandmother treating animals who had sores by smearing them with axle grease which cured of course, in those days you did with what you had and if did not work, were not many more options. I remembered another trick of my grandmothers. She had a dog we called "duke" he could run a rabbit down in a field. The rabbit's only hope was to swerve, the dog going so fast he would run by and have to turn around and resume the chase and sometime could not find the rabbit and sometime could, to the termination of the rabbit. Duke began to get very skinny even though he ate. Grandma told me and my uncle who was only about a year older than me to go to field and find this particular bush which we were very familiar with because if you touch it, it was almost like a burn. We tried to avoid.

She told us to pull bushes and then cut rots off which we did and bring back. The roots were like a small turnip. She peeled the roots and cut into small pieces. Dogs in those days, before dog food, when you threw them food would catch on the fly and go straight down their throat. Never tasted.

After about three days of biscuits and roots, Duke began to gain weight, the root apparently killed worms, if that was problem.

Well anyway, the hairless bulldog I thought needed hair. There were not many dog beauty shops those days and not many girl beauty shops either. We had at the barn a washtub of spent motor oil and remembering the axle grease decided on the grand experiment. I stealthily and conspiringly petted hairless, picked up, carried to barn, and dunked him up to his neck in the used motor oil. He ran but did not yelp. I am sure it did not hurt but in a few months fine hair grew back not as good as original but a nice cover.

A "wag" suggested I should dunk my bald head in it.

When Pug showed up at our house, kids and everybody, she was loved and believed the "dog loved us" it's easy to be loved at our house because when you are loved, it's easy to love.

She lived to a ripe old age and was a joy to have around.

She died of yellow jaundice.

MY RELATIONSHIP WITH GOD

(An elementary view)

My relationship with God became semi-casual in that he never gave me a straight answer, I probably never gave him a straight question but he did say some things that made some sense.

I posed the question to him one day. Well God you are such a smart piece of electronic work, try to grasp this scenario if it is within your electrodes to do so. Here is the scenario.

I began to have these bad headaches and eventually...since you already know all this, they diagnosed Anaplastic carcinoma and you know one thing I discovered God and I want you to explain this to me, why is it that everybody diagnosed with cancer the doctor will look you right in the face and say it is very rare. Why do we really care if it is rare or not. We got it and there is not much we can do about it except listen to what the doctor said, so rarity or not rarity it can be just as devastating and possibly take away the thing we love the most. Well any way this very rare, (1-2 percent) cancer was diagnosed, verified of course you know I am kind of a macho guy and I said what the hell do I care, I am 67 years old anyway and I have about 10 more good years maybe 15, hell the cancer probably won't even remember me, now that it is out and gone or whatever they do with them when they take them out, you don't need to answer that part of the question, what they do with them. So I waltz into the doctor's office at hail-Mayo, I am talking about the Mayo Clinic by any name, it is hail-Mayo because we go in there, cancer patients. We go in there full of piss and vinegar and we immediately know when the doctor looks at us, here's a man that is going to be an exception, we are truly going to save him because he is in good shape physically, he has got a good attitude and most important he has insurance (that's a joke). That is what we all think when we go there, and when you are being treated and you stay at the Mayo weeks and weeks you can spot the ones immediately, they have a different walk, they look different, they dress different but you see them two or three weeks later and they have become just like you because you have been there two or three weeks also. Their walk is not springy, they don't have a sad look but it is definitely melancholy, because they have come to realize they are not any different than the last ten melancholy patients that they meet in the hall. That is a rude awakening because you figured you were different but you are not. I know I was sitting at the table after I had been treating oh, for a couple of weeks and we were all talking, by the way, once you become seriously ill, if you are not extremely cautious it will become the center of your life which is not good. In other words, every conversation you have with anyone else it tends to go back to your illness. That is a very unfortunate way to be. As I said before, sitting at the table with friends and I looked around at all of them, going back to my illness, which maybe something triggered the conversation that way, and I said to them, "if anyone had told me thirty days ago I would be sitting at this table, taking cancer treatments, I would have laughed and rolled on the ground. My idea was that I was invulnerable. My son Duston popped up and said. "I was a little disappointed too because I thought you were superman."

It bothers me a little bit, why God couldn't have made a lot of supermen and I am sure someone is going to say, Oh he did he made thousands of them, millions, of them, he made Hitler, you know, people that have done atrocious things, he made all of them. Of course, the question arises, did he make them do the things they did. Well I don't even want to explain that to me God because you may not have made them do the things they did but allowed it.

Well, superman having found out he is not quite as super as he thought and his face is getting pretty melancholy too, walking down the hall and going to treatment every day at hail-Mayo begins to wonder about some things.

Now, God listen to this real carefully and don't be beeping and having any short circuits or anything like that. I remember the day I came to hail-Mayo with my two sons. I saw four or five doctors which is not even important and don't remember it and I looked at them and I said, "Look (this is before I became a melancholy face) a macho guy like me can handle this crap, I don't need to go through all this radiation and treatment and carp and bull, waste my time down here away from my law practice in Vidalia, just tell me how long I got, if I just do nothing, every doctor at the Mayo said, "Ah, couple of months", now if you don't think that will make superman into a super blubberer you just haven't been there yet.

God or wherever it may come from, puts something in us that still believes that we can do it, we can whip it, we are supermen. That is the biggest fraud ever perpetrated on the human race. We can't do it, we are not supermen but somehow we have got to be able to at least stand up on our haunches and walk down the halls with that melancholy look on our face.

And of course, you immediately (I am sure everybody at hail-Mayo) get hundreds of cards, you get cards from the same people two or three times. It does give you a warm feeling and quite a few of them will say, "We will pray for you", people call you on the phone and tell you, "We will pray for you", then they will give you that standard line, trust in God, he is going to look after you and he is going to bring you through this thing and he is going to take care of you. Well, if there was any trust in God for some of these people here, they would have probably preferred that he would take care of them before they got sick and had to go through the most horrendous, well maybe not the most horrendous but go through a really horrendous regimen.

Now, God I don't really mind if you address that question. What is the logic of a person having this disease assuming, he was trusting in God before he had the disease, then having this life threatening disease and then he is supposed to trust in God to take care of him. Now, we have to assume if a tumor grew in a person or whatever, someone made it grow or some entity could have made it grow or maybe it was a natural thing that happened but if some entity made it grow why should we trust in him to save us after it is removed or to make it die or whatever. I really would like to hear the logic and answer to that question.

Melancholy arises from the frailty of the human spirit.

When the term hail-Mayo is used, it is no reflection on probably one of the finest medical clinics in the world. You have a love-hate relationship with them, they hurt you to help you but you don't have any personal animosity to the doctors it's just one of those things. As you go more and more to hail Mayo you begin to hate where you live near hail-Mayo, you begin to hate the sight of hail-Mayo even though the treatments are basically painless and really no bother to you but you still hate it. A patient that may or may not have gone to hail-Mayo the day she had her last treatment, it had to be the greatest, the greatest rapture that she would ever have in her whole life. I believe that with all my heart.

You realize I am not trying to take up for my frailties in dictating (I love that word frailties by the way) but I think the day the doctors at hail-Mayo told me I had only months to live if I didn't do the treatments my life was changed forever. I must have heard about the thousand people that had cancer and in fact the John Durst Sunday School Class has had at least one person to die from cancer and I may recall some more. I had bad feelings for him but it is nothing like the way you feel once you have done the same thing.

You will never feel the same from that point on when you are diagnosed the way you will feel that another person has been diagnosed. It is like that old feeling when you knew your mother was going to catch you, you knew she was coming, you knew, you had done wrong and you begin to feel warm from your feet up right on up to your stomach, right up into your chest and your head. Your sympathy index has risen considerably. You scream inside for them because you know they are going to soon be screaming and be melancholy. They are at the mercy of hail-Mayo. It is as if you have suddenly gone to Mars, you don't know nothing about nothing, and you don't have a clue what the rules are.

I saw one of my esteemed John Durst Sunday School Class mate at a restaurant and I go up to him, Billy who is one of the finest people ever lived. And of course, I am over the blubbers by now and say, "Hey, Billy, do you think if I had gone to Sunday school more often I wouldn't have gotten this disease and Bill looked right at me and said, Nah, you probably would have gotten it anyway but it might help you get over the disease if you come back." Now, I thought old Billy at that point had both feet on the ground, and of course, he has always been a sharp, quick, guy but that might make a little sense. Not what he said but the concept that it might help me to go back I would have to let you tell me about that God.

PIGTAILS

I went into the fried chicken place to get four cups of coleslaw. I immediately noticed this sort of light skinned black girl that appeared to be about twelve but I am sure she was about 15 or 16. I noticed right away she was very neat, very clean, she had on blue jeans but not like a lot of other teenagers, they were crispy clean, she just looked great. She was the epitome of the scrubbed up little girl who sort of shone throughout, fitness and cleanliness. She had a long pigtail.

I told her I wanted four large cups of coleslaw and as I looked at her she was very serious and I said well, let me see if I can break the ice here, I said I'm sure its about a nickel a cup. She immediately walked over to where they keep a list of what everything costs. She was looking it up. I was really just kidding, it doesn't really matter what it costs but she continued to look it up, "it is not a problem, I was just kidding with you". She still had her mind on what she was doing she was working and she looked at me and said, I just started today. I think what she was saying to me was I just started today and I really want to do a super great job. It could have been her first job but that is just speculation, I have no idea.

Just looking at her and how she looked at you, she was not over-talkative, she had a very reserved innocence and was so proud and I could see that all she wanted to do was to do a good job. It was innocence personified. She was so proud and I know when she got home her mama and/or daddy said, how did the job go? She would gush over with telling, how much she loved it, and how nice everybody was to her and she just wanted to do a good job.

Wouldn't it be wonderful if that innocence continued throughout our lives? To look at our customers, the people we were trying to wait on and all we could think about, this is a wonderful, wonderful thing and I just want to do the very best I can.

Unfortunately, it will all end. The unreasonable customers, the unreasonable boss, the guy or woman who works there and who is way, way past that innocence will do everything they can to destroy the innocence of the person who wants to succeed so bad and loves what she is doing. She hasn't been short changed on her hours by her boss yet, she hasn't been jumped on by one of the customers yet, and she sees the world through innocent eyes which she will never enjoy again the rest of her life. We all remember that first job we had dealing with other people and how it was a great adventure. We will never have that adventure again.

God created innocence but he didn't tell us how to deal with the loss of it. Wouldn't it be wonderful to be the little "I just started girl" behind the counter who looks at you through those innocent wonderful eyes and wants to do the right thing and serve others. How soon we become adversaries and instead of wanting to do the right thing we look at everyone with a certain amount of innocence but we soon realize they are not looking at us the same way. They have an agenda to take advantage of us in some way. Never, never to do the right thing.

What is it that we are all thrust out into the world and our mama's, daddy's and our grandparents have told us what wonderful people we are but they failed to tell us everyone doesn't see us that way. When we go to work as the little pigtail girl did at the fried chicken place, we are wonderful people and we just want to prove it to everyone that comes in the store. Unfortunately most everyone that comes in the store doesn't think we are wonderful people. They are thinking, how can we get our way, how can we play our agenda, how can we take advantage of this situation. There are some that immediately recognize this is a new innocent face and this is an opportunity to take advantage, fortunately most everyone is good and doesn't try that same old option.

I never saw her again in the store after that day. I went in there often and it could have been she just was not working that shift.

I wonder what happened to her. She's probably married and has children but I hope she retained that innocence outlook with the maturity to watch out. I hope she was smart in school and, why not dream, went to college and applied

"looking at the price list", to first day on job.

In my old age, want to see "what happens"
to them. When you are old and have made
average, you can only think about the past, there
is no future to plan for, but it's satisfying to think
about the past and we tend to forget the bad. It
causes nostalgia and a warm feeling to rise up in
yourself.

JAMES DENNIS GROWS UP

Our neighborhood was probably typical, on the north of Vidalia, all on dirt roads. There was the Tapleys, (three boys), Adams, (two boys), one girl who never came out to play and in fact the girls in all the neighborhoods rarely came out to play with the boys.

The immediate neighborhood was at the corner of North Street with Toombs with a little flow over to McIntosh, Orange, and Williford St.

The main players were Ray Adams, Tony Tapley, Donald Williford and James Dennis. All these kids were about 10, a few younger and any older were above being part of our conclave...

There developed an unspoken hierarchy of order. Tony Tapley and Donald Williford were the "big" boys and never fought with one another. Everyone respected that chiefdom except Ray

Adams who beat all the younger kids up every single day except Tony's two younger brother who he knew if attacked would bring on one of the big boys, Tony, who deterred him but not stop trouble and if he could catch Tony not looking, he would hit or push or dare which would usually send one of the young kids crying and running to house and which would bring on retribution by Tony and would cause Ray to leave the scene but he seldom ran crying and I believe never felt defeat because he would do the same thing the next day.

He beat James Dennis up every single day. James had no protector but occasionally one of the big boys would make Ray leave him alone.

Many years after one of the neighborhood kids who was then grown and I could not even remember, said he always like me, because I would not let big kids beat him up.

As it turned out genetics took its course, while James took his licking and would go home in shame after a whipping by Ray and could tell it was humiliating, James took it like a man. There's nothing worse than losing a fight in front of play mates and after over clearly have lost, you kind of shamefully and sheepishly look around hoping for something to be said from playmates or a gesture to help curb humiliation. It seldom comes and you shrink inside and hate yourself and your life, but have to come out and play again. There's nowhere else to go, the neighborhood is the whole world. The real losers never quit get over it and don't want to fight back but this doesn't seem to hurt chances of success in life and in fact some of the aggressors or those who fight back never find their nook in life.

Summers come and go, everyone gets older, and even grew a little and sometime new alliances are forged.

Ray was bigger than most of the kids he picked on but a strange phenomenon happened, everyone continued to grow but Ray stopped. When grown was only about 5'6" and was not husky but skinny and hard as a rock, wirey, knew how to intimidate and bully. He continued to whip up on James.

James continued to grow and was well over 6 feet when grown and was athletic.

Most of the time we played in dirt roads and in the ditches. I shall never forget and it has been over 65 years and can show the exact spot in the ditch on Toombs Street where James Dennis, who was a good head taller than Ray by then, fought back and beat the crap out of Ray. The reign of terror had ended. I never felt such a gushing up in my soul, as I did not like Ray, but thought James was a good guy. If memory serves me James pushed Ray around for several days after ditchgate but then it all stopped.

We were all getting older and went on to other pursuits, playing in the ditch and road was not as much fun anymore. James went on to be a very good football player for the VHS, Ray dropped out of school and had a contentious marriage and life and died young. The Willford's, Palmers, Dennis's, one of the Tapley's, Ray, and his brother, Edward, are all dead.

I often think when driving by those haunts of what my ambition was and it was to get a job making $100.00 per week. When going by, remembering the time we dug a tunnel under a bank in the ditch and it caved in and had to pull digger out by legs. If you could just get a nickel the biggest thrill of all and pray every night, to get a bicycle. My brother learned to ride, it was a Schwinn and came in box and Daddy put it together. The shadows flicker of a time gone by, never to return, and want to say will never be like that again, but it may.

What is that feeling you have when you think of those days and all the people who are gone, get a little teary, but it passes. It's a crying shame.

FATHER'S DAY

(by a father)

I've always been proud of my children, no matter what trouble they got in, always probation.

They always give me shaving lotion and I pour in that 50-gallon barrel out back and it's almost full.

I have a collection of ties that would rival Picasso's greatest works.

They once gave me a gallon of gasoline for my push mower.

They once sacrificed and took time off from busy schedule (play golf on Sunday) to eat a quick lunch on father's day.

They once gave me a burgundy shirt and a white tie. I look like most wanted on poster at post office.

They gave me a bicycle with a ten-coupon payment book.

One thing can say they don't skip on father's day meal, the big tub at KFC.

They never ask for a loan on Father's Day.

Their mother always indulgently looks upon this charade gushing over their remembering and what good children they are.

They always remember father's day two weeks after it happens.

I know they are well adjusted and happy because did not ask for but two loans last year.

They give great advice, wanted me to buy a new car because needed it, and the payments would only be $2100.00 per month.

I know they love me because each has moved into home with children for extended stays on occasion.

Every year for a school fundraiser, sell me a two-dollar pull over shirt for $15.00 that says "Old Guys Rule". I love to wear in public.

They give me their old clothes when Salvation Army turns down.

I know they are the smartest kids in the world because give me advice on how to run my life all the time.

I know they are wonderful and right because mother always takes their side.

They don't ask for forgiveness for any perceived transgression but demand it.

They want to cut my grass but don't have a ride mower.

My daughter married at 18 and divorced before I finished paying for wedding.

My two boys told sister when she announced divorcing that they were not divorcing her husband, instead of brothers in law would become buddies in law.

When married 60 years don't get a divorce; go on parole.

Getting married is like hanging, you just don't ever choke to death.

The most astute statement of this century was "can't we all get along" made by a black guy in California years ago. He might have been troubled but his thoughts were pure, thoughtful, and astute.

Unremarkable would be an upgrade description of my life.

My wife asked me do I have a criminal mind? I married you didn't I.

THE RED FISH

My mother and father made a living selling fish, worms, crickets, and minnow. They also sold boats, motors, boat trailers, and of course, fishing tackle.

My mother was an extremely hard working person and a better businessperson than my father. She worked extraordinarily hard.

She always had a soft place in her heart for people and in particularly for her children and relatives and could see and understand a situation even before it became apparent to others. She had a sense of how others felt, their anxieties, needs, and what was troubling. She just did not miss anything.

After my father died at age 64, heart attack, she went on with/business as usual. Someone ask how do you feel sleeping in marriage bed without

Tap where he had slept for 50 years, her answer "I just go in and go to sleep". I doubt if it is that simple.

When buying minnows for resale sometime get fish other than minnows and sure enough noticed a small red fish who my mother adopted. He grew to six inches and we could look but not bother the red fish. Several people wanted to buy but were refused.

After father died she wanted to sell business and found a buyer who bought her house and the business.

One day she said to me I want you to do something and when my mother asked you to do something you knew it meant something fairly special.

"I want you to take the red fish in a bucket of water and carry to pond behind your house and put him in it". How does God understand that absolute valueless thinking? What kind of person thinks of a lousy red fish? A person with a tender place in her heart not just for a red fish but for everyone.

UNCLE WAFFORD

SOPERTON, GEORGIA

(a near by paradise)

It was a thrill at 9 years old to go to Grandma Brantley's, her name was Tennessee Virginia Tyler and moved to Treutlen County from South Carolina as a young girl to help a relative care for children. She was born in 1892 and died 1974. She met and married George Miller Tapley who was born 1884 and died 1918. They had three children, Denton Duston Tapley, Aldean Hawkins Tapley, and Georgia Tapley, two boys and a girl.

My grandmother on my father's side, Tennessee Virginia Tyler married three times. Her first husband George Miller Tapley, died of the flu that went around the world killing twenty five million about the time of the first world war,

Frank Nathan Page and Tulley Brantley. She buried all three.

1918 was the day of the flu which killed over 25 million people worldwide and a visitor in my office who knew my grandfather, George Miller Tapley, told me that in a small County like Truetlen, he could go to a funeral every day.

We talked about how my grandfather died of the flu. Lore has it, a resident of Truetlen was sent home from service and my grandfather and three others were pallbearers. The casket was opened and all four pallbearers died of the flu including, George Miller Tapley.

At time of his death my grandmother had two little children, Denton and Aldean and pregnant with Georgia. It was desperate times and a young widow pregnant had few options. There were no social organizations to help and no way to "sign up for a check". A reflection of hard times remembered, a few days before Christmas my Grandmother sent me and my uncle Wafford (who was about a year older than me) to a neighbor with a Christmas gift, a shoe box with pecans in it and three or four eggs. We dutifully carried to neighbor, knocked on the door, and handed the box. I believe she was truly thankful.

My grandmother married Frank Nathan Page and had three children by him, Frank Jr., Richard (Dickie), and Wafford. He had been married before and had other children who were grown at time of marriage and were out of household. Mr. Page had land and at his death left all children a farm and the farm my Grandmother lived on was left to her with the understanding eventually to Frank, Dickie, and Wafford. That was the way things were done in those days.

Frank was an abusive husband and some said crazy. At marriage when Grandma came along to the Page farm with three children in tow, it was apparent.

Wafford and I were good friends as well as kinfolks and remember about once a week when I was visiting him the newspaper would come by rural postal carrier and we would spend hours reading the funnies. We would spread the paper on the floor, lay down propped on our arms, and read. A child's satisfaction, fun thing to do, we would read pocket books, and brag we had read them. I remember at Christmas he and I would give a book to each other.

I remember my two boys received from their maternal grandmother a bible for Christmas and watching them out of the corner of my eye, they were holding the books in their hand as if it was a horse turd, not because it was a bible, but a book. The world has changed.

Wafford lived in a log house that was really a big one-room log house where originally everyone lived in that one room. It had a large fireplace in one end and there were two windows, one on each side of fireplace. Facing the fireplace the window on the right was opened by a wood shutter that fit the window to a wood scaffold that held the wood for the fireplace. The fat lighter on the right, hardwood on the left, and no green wood. It was Wafford's job to be sure wood was there every day in the winter

My uncle Wafford and I never had any disagreement except one time when we were in the woods "hunting" came to Pendelton Creek, it was full, and we wanted to cross. There was a foot log which was bobbing up and down and every now and then the water would slightly go over the log, not much, but some. He told me to walk the log to the other side but would not do it, he did not walk it either, but berated me because I wouldn't. It didn't take long for us to make up but I felt unmanly for not walking the log, sort of like a coward.

I could tell when we were going to town on Saturday, my step grandfather would put a tub of water out in the yard for the sun to warm up and he would bath, not in the yard, but bring the tub of warm water in side.

Everyone would put on go "to town clothes". Grand folks would sit on seat up front of wagon and kids would ride on back with feet hanging off wagon. It was quiet an adventure. We would take dirt road as far as could and then get on paved highway. I remember a law passed that all wagons had to have a triangular caution sign on back and grandfather complained of the tyranny of the government.

I remember women sewed then, made clothes, and remember my grandmother looking at sacks of flour that were printed in a design with idea to sew something. I remember the old superstition to do what you enjoy most on New Year's day because that is what you will be doing for the rest of year. My Grandmother sewed.

I remember we would go to town, Soperton on Saturday and stay all day. We would go in the wagon with grownups and everybody put their mule and wagon behind the stores where there was a water trough and corn or hay was carried to feed the mule. It was an adventure because going to town with Wafford was a treat. We would run all over town looking in windows and looking at people. The smell was heady. I lived in town, Vidalia, but it was different in Soperton with

Wafford. Wafford was given a whole dollar to spend; my parents gave me a quarter. He got a dollar because he worked the farm turpentine on halves. We would load up on junk, go to movie, and see both features.

After movie would buy a hamburger and had to buy through a window that opened out to sidewalk. They sold beer where hamburgers were made and kids couldn't go in.

Wafford had two dogs, Rover and Duke. Rover was the fighter and boss, Duke could run and run a rabbit down on the fly.

I remember Duke began to lose weight (he was always skinny) and realized something was wrong. I remember Gramma told us to go to field and look for this particular bush. I had seen it many times, it had thorns that when you touched felt like fire.

She told us to dig up bush and bring root back to her.

Dogs in those days if you threw something to eat would swallow whole, seldom tasting. She took a piece of the root, put in a biscuit and threw to Duke, which he swallowed whole without tasting. She did this for about three days and Duke began to gain weight.

Gramma said he had worms, which the root killed. It appeared to be true.

HE SHOT THE DOG

I remember the day Uncle Wafford and I hitched up the wagon and headed to the rocks, an area where rocks cropped up out of the ground forming a cliff, which looked like the Rocky Mountains, or so we pretended so. Some time we would build a fire under a ledge by taking a tar cup from tree which burned real good. We would pretend we were cowboys like in the movies where the cowboys were always around rocks. It was one of our favorite play places.

A white dog had taken up at Gammas, very friendly fellow and went everywhere Wafford and I went. Wafford already had two dogs, Duke and Rover. Unbeknownst to me this would be a traumatic day not for me particularly but for Wafford, I had no clue.   He was probably about 10 years old and me about the same.

We went near the rocks in the wagon and I was sitting on the seat and Wafford got out and took his rifle. By that time the dogs had stopped and were around the wagon wagging tails, "where we going next, waiting to see". The dogs were looking at us expectantly, anxious to be on the way.

Wafford took his rifle and propped up on back of wagon, turned to new dog, aimed dog was looking expectantly, tail wagging anxiously ready to be on way. I can't remember if I knew what was going to happen or not. He shot the dog, a pet. It never moved but fell on side, dead.

It was traumatic for me and looked at Wafford, who swallowed hard, his face ashen, before this time had never seen that look on his face and never saw it again but the lump remained in his throat for his life. The tough and who cares face was gone forever, he appeared to be in shock and I was so taken aback, my stomach felt funny, and a hot dread came over me.

All this took place in seconds. The tough, never a care attitude of Wafford tried to return but could tell he couldn't quite do it. He got on wagon and nothing was said until he made some sort of a sideways remark that dog wasn't any good anyway and nobody cared about him. He and I cared, at least me, and found out over seventy years later, Wafford cared.

Seventy years later taking to Donna, his wife after Wafford's death, she told me Wafford never got over that time and agonized over it. His tough exterior wasn't so tough inside. Wafford told her that dog looked at him "I love you, why, what have I done? He mentioned that trauma to her 50 years later and she told me he never got over it. At 83 years old, I remember it well.

I would never have thought Wafford gave another thought to shooting of the dog. I was around him for 50 years thereafter and he never mentioned under that supposingly invulnerable shell of the man's exterior was a soul of a boy who loathed to shoot a worthless dog and cried inside for doing it.

What is inside us that causes the agony of shooting a worthless dog who did not even have a name? Whatever it is it seems to have gone out of the human race who blithely abandoned their children who aren't even lowly dogs. We, myself and Wafford had something inside us whether learned or whatever God there may be gave to us. That is the creator given feeling unknown that even animals have. That, whatever Wafford and myself felt that day and carried all our life is an unknown quantity that separates the good from the bad. It is sad we don't all feel that way. As humans we need to feel sorry for that dog, that elephant, that lion, that turtle, and that child who needs us.

I begin to notice Wafford was not as interested in running "all over town" as he got older. I began to realize he was not as interested in my coming out in the county to visit him which to me was a super treat. He began to have friends that had their "pa's" car. (Nobody had driver licenses then, you just drove, kids and all)

I had no yearnings in this new direction, reading the funnies satisfied my cravens. I soon realized that Wafford and his new friends with the car were after "women". The women didn't look like near as much fun as running all over town and buying hamburgers through the window. I found out later they were a lot more fun.

We kinda went our separate ways along about then, he was becoming a man and I was still adolesceing. He moved and went in the air force, I meander thought high school and it appeared would be drafted, Korean Conflict, so volunteered for draft and went into the army for two years, went to University of Georgia, got out of army 22 days early to enter College, anything to get out of Army, saw Wafford off and on he finally settled with four children in Albany, Ga. This female, that I didn't in the past think was much fun, cajoled me into marrying her, but it is not going to work and have decided to call it quits after 60 years. That is a long time with one woman.

Wafford's wife called and said he had been in an accident and was in the hospital and apparently paralyzed from waist down. He told me he was standing in water about waist deep and was going to dive and grab wife's feet and duck her. He bumped ever so lightly his head when dived and was paralyzed for life. He was 30 years old, had all ideas he would be cured, and walk again but not to be. I have noticed that every person paralyzed believes they will walk again and wonder when realize it's not going to happen.

He moved to Vidalia and we took up where let off when reading the funnies on the floor propped up on arms.

There are many complications of being paralyzed and sitting in a wheel chair for 25 years. There were many adventures we had around the wheel chair mostly dreamed up by Wafford. He had a lot of time to think just sitting there.

His medical problems were many but never lost his sense of humor but became very dictatorial and have noticed persons in wheel chairs become that way, demanding that it be done and their judgment is always right. His wife Donna was the blunt of most of his demands. She struggled and only a super human could take care of him like she did. He drank constantly, beer being his choice, always saying the doctor recommended it, good for the kidneys and persons in wheel chairs have kidney problems. He finally went on dialysis toward the end.

There were humorous times. I was constantly there and remember one time the family called saying he was out of his gourd and wanted me to come. It was about ten pm, went, and the family thought his kidney function had gone bad and needed to go to VA hospital, which he refused to do. When I arrived, against his wishes, told his boys to put him in van and with him complaining headed for VA hospital in Augusta, stating he was not going in hospital and began to take off his clothes. When arrived at hospital he was sitting in wheel chair naked, saying again he was not going in, I instructed his boys to take out of van and push naked in wheel chair into admitting room. I apologized to receptionist for his nakedness but when pushed him to her desk she could not see and just continued to fill out admitting papers. When completed stood up for signatures and stated, "he is naked isn't he" It was humorous afterwards. He went into hospital and completely recovered denying he would ever do such a thing.

We cooked out all the time, my two boys admired him and he was a lovable and funny character most of the time. Everyone thought he was a character and he was. He sent me with his oldest son to buy the son a car and he and I had in mind a four door family type. The son insisted on a Dodge Charger and when Wafford saw car had only one comment, "I would get mine when my sons wanted a car". Wafford was a funny guy. He was often in Veteran's hospital and remember told he was in operating room, and doctor came in and said to him "I should cut that thing off referring to his penis," Wafford's retort was, gesturing with finger across neck, "cut it off here".

If you bought a new pair of shoes, "he would always say where'd you get the new "kicks".

He always said if you had a full tank of gas and ten bucks in your pocket, "life ain't too bad."

I thought at time he was tyrannical to his wife and children but they were loyal.

When he died selected a black preacher friend to give his funeral, which was in character for him, and the eulogy was wonderful. I will never forget the example of how Wafford left the station on the train many times for a final ride but the preacher's train always returned to station, but this time it did not return. Wafford would have liked that.

It was a long growing up relationship and often thought of him and knew he had not changed wherever he is. I'll be getting on that train in the not too distance future and hope it returns a couple of times to the station.

PHALLUS ENVY

We have in this society several sub species of humanoids, not talking about color or race. We have males and females, females who do not know if they are males, males who do know if they are females, females who know they are males, and males who know they are females.

They base this gender snafu on their leanings, yearnings, and what their heart tells them. The last time my heart whispered to me, it told me I was a worthless ugly piece of crap, who had BO(body order), bad teeth that were seldom brushed, who had no direction, no worthwhile feelings, my tattoos were smeared, didn't know which one was my father and wanted to look at naked women. I deny the first seven, hell, nobody's perfect.

To a boy from South Georgia all this is confusing. He always thought if you stripped off naked and looked into a mirror (frontal view) you got a pretty good idea what gender you were.

The biggest problem we have in this society all females want one of them things like boys have. From the day bathed with a boy as a child it has been an item of curious fascination.

Females know they will always sit on the left hand of God while all those guys with one will sit on the right hand of God. After all, his only begotten son had one, we think.

Woman block this phallus envy by over responding to males, who have one. They are defensive and rather than accuse the male with one of being a male with one, they circle the wagons shooting as one rides by for no apparent reason except the shootee has one.

The most crushing unfulfillment are the persons who are concerned about who they are sexually, will never enjoy the greatest God given pleasure to mankind that is normal pleasurable encounter with a person of the opposite sex, resulting in a sexual encounter and the problematic climax. Sex is the most driven of all our desires and is the mechanism by which man remains on this earth.

We hunt, fish, and work with the goal that it will lead to procreation of the species and one of the most pleasurable experiences that God had divined on us.

Think what a dirty trick God has played on those who do not know if they are a girl or boy. God sure played a joke on them.

There are other fulfillments but if can't taste sugar, it's hard to substitute or explain to another what they are missing.

BARK UNDER HIS TONGUE

I knew Clyde Dykes when we were in high school in Vidalia, Georgia. He was one grade ahead of me.

Clyde was a good-looking guy and very athletic. He came from a large family but I can't remember what his father did for a living. A story he told me over and over was how his mother picked cotton to buy him clothes for school. He never forgot and often spoke highly of his mother as all good southern children do. He never forgot and for the uninitiated picking cotton was a bag around your neck, which you dragged down the row and plucked the cotton from boles and put in your bag. It was hot, dirty sweaty sandspury, beggar lice work but if could pick 100 lbs in a day, that was Olympian, but the reward was lofty, $3.00 dollars per hundred. It was honorable employment and often the owners of the cotton patch would feed everybody lunch (it was called dinner then)

I really got to know Clyde when went to work at Piggly Wiggly in Vidalia, he was a stocker and bag boy. I worked in the meat market. None of us had cars but Clyde saved enough money to buy a 39 Ford and we were going to Pembroke to see some girls but about halfway to Lyons from Vidalia a rain storm hit, Clyde had wipers but in those times wipers worked off a vacuum and if you accelerated by pressing the gas the wipers stopped. We did not make it to Pembroke.

After graduation, Clyde went full time with Piggly Wiggly and became the youngest store manager in Piggly Wiggly history. He later became a supervisor over several stores, company furnished a car, he was doing really good.

A problem arose when, gossip was he became enamored over a cashier at a store in Augusta and it goes without saying, she was a looker, sort of a playmate, Miss August, Piggly Wiggly asked him to resign, but, several big grocery companies tried to hire him.

Clyde married Miss. August, she came with a daughter, and he raised her. At the time of the marriage, Clyde had purchased a "Mom and Pop" grocery store in Lyons, Georgia. The grocery store prospered and life was good except Clyde worked about 25 hours a day, but work was no stranger to him. The stepdaughter finished school and college on Clyde's dime.

When stepdaughter went off to College in North Carolina Miss. August went with her leaving Clyde all alone. He became seriously ill and was not able to run store or really take care of himself. He denied to me, but knew he asked Miss August to come back and help him but she would not. Clyde had raised the daughter and she got everything she wanted and when went off to college, Miss. August went with her Clyde paid for daughters' schooling, Miss August went to work for a big bank and Clyde would brag to me how many promotions she had and was moving up fast. She had the "personality" to move up.

She did not call to see about him but one time, the Bank had repossessed a Mercedes and wanted Clyde to send money and buy for her. I did their divorce and talked Clyde into giving her zilch. He approached me later about signing the stock in corporation over to her, which was the business. I absolutely hit the glass ceiling

Jumping ahead of the "bark" when Clyde died Miss August showed up with daughter in tow and in discussing the estate I mentioned there were just the three boys and Miss August chimed in there were 4, Clyde had adopted the daughter but never mentioned to me because knew I would not approve.

When went to store at time of marriage to meet Miss August for first time, I had a first impression of her, it was not a good impression and proved to be a correct impression. First impressions are usually correct. One person wrote a whole book on the topic of first impressions and determined by experiments the first impression is usually right. I had a first impression of her and was right. She never loved Clyde and wanted what she could get out of him.

Clyde knew in his heart the truth of the matter.

When Clyde was sick, his sister took him to her home and cared for him. Clyde never forgot and when she became disabled, he took sister to his home, hired 24-hour care, and took care of her until her death.

Clyde did everything in store and I mean everything. One of the chores was unloading truck with grocery supplies and carrying into store. On this particular day were unloading boxes of chickens packed in ice, weighed about 70 pounds. The truck was being unloaded through a side door. The driver would put chickens on floor of truck and Clyde would lift and put on dolly. The chicken boxes were stacked on top of each other in truck about six high.

As Clyde was placing a box on dolly but had not placed on dolly, a box of chickens from top of stack in truck fell striking him on back before he had placed box in hands on dolly. The blow broke the biceps muscle in arm, broke muscles in the rotator cuff, and injured his back. He underwent several operations but the bicep muscle could not be repaired and he was left with a "pop eye" muscle. He was never quite the same person after injury.

The wholesale company refused to accept liability and Clyde sued. The trial was held in Statesboro, Judge Nevils, presiding. The jury found for the grocery company, that's a story in itself. It was a long ride from Statesboro to Vidalia after jury verdict. Clyde and I did not have a lot to say.

Motion was made for new trial and Judge Nevils granted, stating "the case was well presented and there was a real injury".

We went back tried case again and were awarded $125,000.00. We had a lot to talk about going home that day.

In talking Clyde said, "I knew we were going to win". I had had a few beers by that time and asked "What do you mean you knew we were going to win?" I prayed but knew in my heart he had not bribed a juror.

He explained went to witch (we called her) doctor in Toombs County and ask for her help. "She gave me a piece of bark and told me to put under tongue when went into court room and leave until trial was over". He reached in mouth and took piece of bark out. I laughed but it was kind of a nervous chuckle.

I knew exactly who Clyde was talking about and had been by her house many times and saw the cars parked, and people there seeking her help and many folks swore by her magical powers. I was becoming a believer rapidly and actually represented her in an estate matter. She was a very nice person and business was business with her.

Clyde was one in a million, a loyal employee of Piggly Wiggly (people at Piggly Wiggly were like a family) knew what hard work was about, and lived by the creed, the reward is doing the right thing, work honestly, and be thankful of the opportunity to earn by working. In my life, that philosophy was killed by hit and run in the early hours of the morning.

THE FIRST NEIGHBORHOOD

When we moved to Vidalia about 1943, before WWII was over we moved to the end of McIntosh Street in one-half of house. The Mosley's lived in the other half. I don't remember much about them but were pleasant except Ralph often had a disobedience problem with mother. He was older than us. It was a street with two lanes divided by Palms in the middle. I remember when the palms were done away with and the Street widened with a dividing line down middle my father saved two of the palms and one survives at 509 Peach tree in the yard... Through the years both trees were frozen back but always recovered. The one left looks very good but am sure someone will want to do away with it. I don't recall what happened to the other.

Humble beginnings, I remember going to school and after seating the teacher would ask each student to stand up and give their name, street address and telephone number. I was always embarrassed because we did not have a phone. Another embarrassing thing is when it rains the school had what was called a half session. Usually lunch was out for one hour or so everyone could go home to eat. There were no buses and no lunchroom. On rainy day if there was no one to pick you up you stood on steps under the roof. It was embarrassing because then everyone would know your family did not have a car. I remember one rainy day I was so mad decided to get revenge on my mother and on way home after rain had stopped, got under a down pipe where water was coming out and got soaked, that'll teach my mom to come pick us up. Mom did not seem too upset, which was disappointing.

The first day of school, we were carried to school and parents told us where we would be living and told us to ask someone how to get to the new house. I remember Jerry Wilkes lived in neighborhood and showed us where we lived. It was a good neighborhood Emmett Allmond lived across the street and spent several happy hours playing at his house. His mother would always give us a cookie and sometimes in the winter a cup of soup. It was a heady time. Everyone had a chicken pen. We were afraid to go in. Emmetts' hen pen because the rooster would chase you.

An oddity about playing out in those times were the girls rarely came out to play, Emmett had a sister Emily, they were twin, and she never came out to play and noticed other girls did not come out to play with the boys. Mr. Allmond drove a taxi and had a green Fraser automobile. We lived across the street for several years and don't believe Mr. Allmond ever said a word to me, not that he was unkind, but that was the way things were, you were not a grown up, and did not speak if not spoken to.

We finally got a lunchroom at school, lunch was 25 cents. Everyone complained about the food but me, it was a mile to walk from home and back for lunch.

About once a week, lunchroom would have biscuits. If you got up to get something, left your plate, when you came back your biscuit had vaporized. David Fowler was an enterprising fellow and later became president of the senior class. When he got up and left his plate and the vulnerable biscuits, I remembered well the first time he stood up, and realized by some psychic mystery his biscuits would not be there on his return. He picked up the biscuits spit on them, rubbed spit around, with fork on biscuits and on return his biscuits were intact and in-place.

There was temperate adventure at Vidalia High School, things were simple then, it was a heavy embarrassment to get caught cheating, cheating is a way of life now and if can cheat and get by, more power to you. We should try to go back to being embarrassed.

RUMONATIONETTES

I remember riding down through the hallowed streets of Lyons, Georgia with my wife, who suffers from Alzheimer's and we passed the house where she lived when we married, and I said look we are passing your old house, where we smooched on the couch and I tried to feel you up. Her response, "what were you feeling for?" I almost said, "can't remember".

Another time recently sitting on the couch, I raised up to ease relief from sitting on my gonads, and wife asked what are you doing? I answered relieving pressured from sitting on my balls, she said, what balls?

My wife asked me to help find something she couldn't find. What are you looking for? Wife, I don't know but can't find it. Husband, its hard to find something if don't know what it is are looking

for, we both burst out laughing.

HERMAN MOORE

We lived next door to Herman and Hazel Moore. They had three boys, younger than me and my two brothers. We had a 'basketball goal' in our back yard and Herman would come over to play with us on occasion, he was a big basketball star and had played at Collins, Georgia. He shot the ball under handed, which others did also at the time. How basketball has changed.

Herman worked as a fireman for the railroad company he worked at night shoveling coal in a locomotive furnace. All night long, they switched cars around. Herman was the hardest working person on the face of the earth and had a second job working as a meat cutter for Piggly Wiggly, Sims Stores on Saturday.

As progress would have it some enterprising MBA (Master of Business

Administration) from Harvard decided it would be much cheaper for the rail road to change the coal fired engine to a diesel engine which is less a chore than shoveling coal into engine furnace.

Survival of the fittest, coal shovelers, decided the railroad should pay them as fireman to turn the diesel fuel handle. That had as much chance of success as the proverbial snowflake in hell.

Herman, not because he was a particularly MBA Harvard person, but had that good old commodity, south Georgia common sense, hard work pays, there are no free brunches but are earned by good old hard work, it helps if you like it, and knowing you have done your best because that's the right way, it's the way you are raised.

He went fulltime with Piggly Wiggly after Rail Road and retired after about 100 years of service. They probably made him retire. He wanted to always work.

My parents always on the lookout for ways to torture their children conned Herman into hiring his oldest, Tony, to work in the meat market in Lyons, Georgia. He was 13 years old and that was the first real job he ever had.

Herman was funny about some things, for one, he expected you to work. You started at day light and worked until 11 at night but the money was good $3.00 dollars a day. A Saturday with Herman was about fifteen hours and the thing was he did it and expected you to do it. He taught me how to work by example and even at that young age grungily admired Herman and many years after admired and respected him even more for the man he was.

I shall never forget found out the bag boys were making $4.00 dollars per Saturday and working about three hours per Saturday less than me. (one of those bag boys later became a helicopter pilot and retired from service, he was a good looking guy about three years older than me, had an automobile, and set a world record for driving to Vidalia from Lyons and back in fifteen minutes on a two lane highway in lunch hour traffic. It was exciting and at that age there is no danger.

I approached Herman about this "atrocity" of injustice ($3. 00/ $4.00) would have thought the way he carried on about that dollar, had asked him to shoot his mother but he gave it to me. In the society of Saturday, bag boys the going rate was $4.00 per day except at Morris Foods in Vidalia, $5.00 per day, top of the line. I remember also how the bag boys at Morris Foods would brag about stealing rolls of change from Mr. Morris.

I worked there until about the tenth grade when Herman told me his brother needed a job and mine was the job he needed but he had arranged for me to work at the new super Piggly Wiggly in Vidalia and was paid $6.50 per Saturday for shorter hours. I had assented. Bob Humphrey was the market manager and a great guy.

It was a different world there. They had a small self-service for wrapped meat but still mainly waited on customers individually.

I met the people who later became the president and vice presidents of a growing Piggly Wiggly company and when graduated from high school was offered a full time job.

I went to work for my dad who was a foreman with a construction company. My ascension had stopped, it was hard convict labor for about 30.00 per week but was saved again when a fellow classmate called and wanted to know if would go to work as a lifeguard at new swimming pool in Vidalia at $37.50 per week. I knew how to swim so took job. I had died and gone to heaven. Women were everywhere in bathing suits, not the skimpy kind like now, but skimpy enough to trigger the imagination. I was one of the first guards to ever work at pool.

Unfortunately summer ended, the job ended, and my prospects of being drafted in the Army exponentially increased.

I was drafted but when the North Koreans heard of my induction, an Armistice was reached. Another stroke of good luck. Several of the skimpy bathing suits wrote to me in Army but soon went on to a guy with a better tan.

The point of all this backstroking through life was Herman Moore, an icon, who started me on the way by example of honesty, hard work, good humor, and the job he gave me taught me how to deal with people. Even after he retired, he went to work part time for a hardware store. I often wondered if the hardware store owners knew what they had in Herman Moore. He was a man of good spirits and a living example of what God meant to create.

HAVE YOU SEEN BETTY

I don't think she slept in her bed last night and did not see her when I got up.

I don't think she went jogging with me although felt a presence and look beside me to the left and right but did not see anything. Maybe she was overhead.

Where can the essence of Betty be? Know if she could be with us, she would and we can only speculate wherever she is she does not have in her being to be with us.

I wonder if she realizes that she is not with us and does she want to be. We must believe she wants to be with us and probably cries when can't. We cry when we want, to no avail when she is not there.

Does God really want us to suffer, nah, he is a good God and wants us all to be happy, maybe if we ask, it will let Betty come back.

I scream inside for him to answer and let Betty come back or let us know where she is, if she is anywhere.

Silence, silence, there is not a sound except the crying inside and it hurts. We can hope that where Betty is she is not crying and is not hurting.

We can hurt for all of us.

Do we really feel a presence or is there really a presence, we can only imagine.

Why does this purported God make us needlessly suffer, it brings on nothing. Alas, is this part of our repentance to enter that veiled place called heaven. It doesn't make any sense to have to suffer to be with it in paradise.

I call it because what exactly are these Gods we all so grandly believe in. I personally have never heard from any of them. Will it be a bass or baritone voice? I've seen it in the movies or was that the real thing.

It is such a little thing, couldn't we just have some word from Betty. I would like to find out if am going to paradise or perhaps we could have a little paradise on earth.

I suppose could wait a little longer to hear from Betty it has only been about ten years, of course if have to want for ten more will probably be where she is if she is anywhere.

When you arrive at the facility, she takes your hand, holds if for hours, and won't turn loose. What is she thinking and what are you thinking. Has it, God, totally forgotten children and those like Betty who aren't home don't deserve it. They are as innocent as those lambs," bringing in the sheaves", B.S. We are totally alone but it would be wonderful if we were not alone.

We can up our tithing, that'll do it. Have you heard the one, where preacher comes in and tells wife have been offered ten thousand more per year, to move to a new church, tells wife going to study and pray, ask God what need to do and you start packing.

We all need to start packing.

Photo taken January 9, 1945 showing General Douglas MacArthur fulfilling his promise of "I shall return" to the Philippines. In photo to the left of MacArthur is Sgt. Glenn Brooks who was killed in action approximately 10 days after photo was taken. He was the husband of Flossie Brooks reference in story Flossie Draft Notice

FLOSSIE - DRAFT NOTICE

I remember when they came to my mother's first cousin's house, after dark. A knock, because on those days houses were not well lit, but tended to be lighted where the source of light was a lamp or after REA a single bulb in the middle of the room, with most of the house in shadows. Every one tended to sit around light or at fireplace in winter and even after cold weather at fireplace or around the kitchen table after eating and clean up.

The kids oblivious to everything except playing, running over house and being noisy, but you were not loud enough to disturb to any degree the adults. It was understood behavior.

World War II was on and many relatives were missing mostly young boys who had been drafted. In those days, if drafted and notice to meet at a place usually somewhere down town, Soperton, where there would be several draftees and all were transported together in a bus to a base to be to be examined and inducted in army. At ever send off a member of the draft board had to be there to send all off and wish good luck, God speed, etc, sort of like I am sending you to die but am man enough to look in face and tell you it is for the good of the country, I'd like to go, but have to stay and practice air raid drills and be sure every house closes blinds at night so the enemy with planes cannot see lights and bomb Soperton.

A draft board member must come and tell you to your face your son or husband was killed in action. A duty not relished by many.

The knocker asked for Flossie Brooks and she dutifully came to door, was about 20 years old. The knocker said something to her and handed her some papers, she began to cry softly holding her head down in her hands. I watched this with wondering bewildering curiosity and felt funny inside seeing an adult cry and particularly Flossie who was the pretties and nicest relative.

The family came to see what the matter was and began to hold her. The door was still open and knocker stood in door with a sorrowful sympathetic helpless look on face, sad shuffling, with hands in pocket.

That was 72 years ago and I shall never forget what that feeling a child has inside seeing a grownup loved, suffer its inside and no particularly place but a warm dread somewhere in chest and stomach.

The picture shows husband to the left of McArthur with holstered pistol. He was killed two weeks later.

THRUSH

My grandmother came to Soperton when about 14 years old to live with relatives who lived out from Soperton, South, down on the River, where all the Barnhill's lived. She went to the relatives to help care for little children. The total circumstances of exactly why she went are not fully known. She always said many years later she was there to help care for children. It is not known if she ever returned to see mother and father again. She was from South Carolina and a trip those days with no real transportation would have been long and hard. There were no cars and it is not known how she came from South Carolina to Soperton. Her name was Tennessee Virginia Tyler.

She married George Miller Tapley in 1912, she was 20 years old, he was 28. They had three children, Denton Duston Tapley, Aldine Hawkins

Tapley and Georgia Tapley. She was pregnant with Georgia Tapley when George Miller Tapley died of the flu in 1918. Lore has it he was a pallbearer along with three others, casket was opened, all the pallbearers died of the flu. Everyone knows of the flu epidemic that killed millions about that time. A person from Soperton told me, who knew my granddaddy, George Miller Tapley, that in the small town of Soperton he could go to a funeral every day because of the flu.

In those times, there was no help for a widow with two small children and one on the way. It isn't clear what happened after death of George Miller Tapley but very soon thereafter Gramma married Frank Nathan Page and moved to his farm near Gillis Springs, north of Soperton. He had grown children who had left home.

She had three children by Nathan Page, Wafford, Dickie, and Frank. He died very early in the marriage, Wafford and Dickie were young boys. Frank had struck out on his own.

My Aunt Georgia married and had four children, three boys and a girl. Aunt Georgia lived in Vidalia and that's where the children were raised.

Along about then babies would come down with a mouth disease called thrush. It was extremely painful and baby would cry continuously, could not sleep, or nurse. It was traumatic to baby and parents to say the least.

There is at least one family member who remembers her child who is now grown coming down with thrush. How can you treat a small child that can't even sit up in 1950?

Word spread there was a woman who lived in Vidalia who could cure a child's thrush by blowing in its mouth. It was Georgia Tapley Barwick.

The mother of the child who was carried to Georgia Tapley Barwick is alive and will verify, she carried the child, Barwick blew in its mouth, the thrush went away shortly thereafter. The child who is now grown lives in Toombs County. There were many who carried children to her. Barwick has been long deceased. There would often be several cars at her house with children who had thrush.

We think this is a strange phenomenon but in the book, The Egyptian, about an Egyptian doctor, who doctored the Pharaoh and who actually did operations. This was a time when Pyramids were being built. The doctor had a blood "stopper" who which when an incision was made the "stopper" could actually make the person stop bleeding. Unfortunately, they both had a run of bad luck, the doctor was the Pharaoh's doctor and the Pharaoh died and now follows the sun across the sky in his golden chariot. Unfortunately, when the Pharaoh died his treating doctor had to be put to death by beheading alone with his "stopper". When their heads were laid on the block and the sword went down to chop, the executioner stopped just at the neck, the doctor had been symbolically executed. Unfortunately, the "stopper" did not know this and died of fright, heart attack, whatever. One blood stopper lost to prosperity.

I can report two things about Aunt, Georgia died of old age and when never failed to cure the thrush, while there may have been disappointments, she was not symbolically executed.

We don't know about the blood "stopper" but to have the ability to cure the thrush, the person who can cure must had been born after the death of the father.

Georgia Tapley Barwick was born after her father died of the flu.

MOTHER

You look at a picture of yourself when you were 13 years old and stare at your eyes and wish you could look behind those clear eyes, what is behind them and what were you thinking.

Your skin is young, lips full, no wrinkles, a slight smile on your face and you think of your mother and how wonderful she was to you, unrequited love, and she asked so little of you then.

I remember one time my mother ask me to sweep and mop the kitchen which was about a 10 x 10, a 5 minute job and you are giving her a hard time and resistance and "why can't you sweep and mop" and she finally says I'm going to have a baby and slight guilt slips in, it was such a little thing.

There is not one person in this world that would not like to go back to their mother and grab her and say I'd be very pleased if you would let me sweep and mop the kitchen ten times over.

I feel it's a punishment to not be able to do this simple thing. The greatest mystery of life, will we ever see them again? Can we ever redeem our self? The funny thing is mother does not seek redemption she understood you were a child and would be proud you would want to sweep and mop her kitchen. She has raised a good child who longs to sweep and mop her kitchen, such a small thing. The boundless sentiment that comes straight from whatever Gods there may be, not earned, but given.

Let me hug her one more time.

I SHALL NEVER FORGET YOU

It was nothing but ignorance and old age; I had put my papers on the top of my car and forgot to put them in my car after opening the door. Needless to say leaving and accelerating on the highway cause the papers to blow off and scatter over the highway. I realize this after going about one hundred feet and looking back saw my "life" work scattered to the four winds all over the highway. I immediately turned off and ran back to gather papers up, it was quiet a mess. As I ran pell mell over the road a silver SUV stopped and blocked traffic to stop further scattering.

She was an attractive woman about 25, blonde hair and a ready smile with kind sad eyes. Very attractive eyes.

As she handed me the papers her smile was kind, she had nice lips and light colored eyes, a high forehead, I said to her "I shall never forget you" and she smiled kindly with a radiant amused countenance that spoke, I love people and show my love by helping others such as those who need immediate help and am pleased to do because I am a kind person, because that's what God wanted me to be, and serve goodness and kindness and the kindness returned not because deserved it but it's for all of us.

God gave us something not measurable but a feeling of what's right, what is my goodness that propels me to act this way.

The child who holds his arms up wanting nothing but to be held, loved, and squeezed not knowing why he wants but an inner desire, just as the girl who helped pick up the papers.

What mystery that will never be explained and needs no explanation for the warm feeling that comes over us, a satisfaction that defies any explaining and needs none.

Pick up those papers today for someone and the feeling will be a warmth that floods over us, a God given sensation.

A MESS OF MULLET

Clyde Carter told me this story 50 years after it happened. The family lived in a rough wood house heated by a fireplace with water drawn from a well, wood shuttered windows, kerosene for lighting and an outhouse. Just about like everyone else. A penny in a child's hand was a small fortune just waiting to get to town and spend, after extensive shopping and looking. You don't rush to spend that kind of money.

He had several brothers and sisters who never got that far from home.

In those days, no one had any money and farmers would hire folks to gather crop, primarily cotton, and pay hands after cotton was sold. It worked pretty good and everyone eagerly awaited the sale and payment. If, worked enough that may bring two or three dollars, an absolute fortune.

Farmer Caine asked mama would she and children pick cotton to be paid when cotton sold. It was a Godsend, she anxiously agreed, and she and children picked several weeks all day long, to be paid by poundage. Mama and kids felt blessed. It was funny Clyde never mentioned his daddy and if so I have forgotten.

There was not one day passed when we didn't ask mama how long did she think before cotton sold, she would laugh and told us not to bother her or ask again but we could tell her face lit up when we would ask.

The magic day came and here came farmer Cain, we could hardly contain ourselves. He gave mama a mess of mullet and left. I heard mama crying in the house, a hot feeling rose up inside me, a combination of dread and hate.

Clyde never forgot and vowed to never let that happen again. He would succeed and have all of everything he wanted. He did succeed and became semi wealthy. His brother Estus became very wealthy.

He married a good solid woman similar to his background, who knew the value of a dollar. They both worked hard. Clyde took a government job and made a decent salary and made much money as a result of job. He never forgot that mess of mullet.

They had no children, adopted, one good boy and one sorry one. Clyde would buy a car always a mercury and drive for ten years and it looked as good after ten years as day bought. He was very close with his money.

One day he said to me he was thinking of buying a Cadillac but just could not make up mine, too rich for his blood. I said you should buy a Cadillac, when you go to nursing home and sitting on Christmas day rocking on the porch, your son is going to drive up in a Cadillac purchased with your money, hand you a Christmas gift of cheap shaving lotion which can put with other 200 gallons accumulated through the years, wish you a Merry Christmas, stay five minutes, and apologize for rushing off but just has to go and take care of some business. Clyde bought a Cadillac that day.

Clyde suffered a stroke later in life which did not disable him but changed his shrewdness, his wife died, and he married high school sweet heart.

He loaned money at exorbitant rates and dealt with locals but as his fame spread others came who offered big rewards. They had handled a few messes of mullet.

He lost big and almost in an export/import scheme may have broken the law (not drugs) he escaped but suffered a big loss.

He died not broke and relatively happy. His high school sweet heart married a man of God, don't know how happy she is. His sorry son died after squandering what Clyde left him and I don't know where the good son is or what he is doing.

Clyde never took his eye off that mess of mullet.

RENAISSANCE JUDGES

I remember starting the practice of law in 1977 not knowing exactly what was doing but didn't take long to almost find out. Those lawyers that did know what they were doing were good at giving lessons usually leaving scars but for every scar, you helped other lawyers and gave them a scar.

I hardly knew how to draw a lawsuit but another lawyer just said tell a story and that seem to do the trick. We did not have copiers and used carbon paper and try to imagine drawing a commercial 10-page lease using carbon paper. I bought first copier, Xerox, which would make one copy at the time. It cost $4000.00 and bought a better copier and printer at a local Chinese stocked merchandise Mart for $100.00. Of course it only copies and prints in Chinese. You get what you pay for.

Lawyers are not a bad crowd and its what clients want that bring on bad reputation. They want results and care little about who is destroyed and mained to get it. Lawyers have to eat too (prefer raw meat) so they destroy Granma and take her house putting her under an oak tree to live out "golden" years. That sounds mercenary but that's what lawyers do but the next time trouble comes along call a plumber to handle it.

An integral part of law is the judges and remember when started most judges were gruff, unkind, talked down to you, and generally treated you like an inconvenience that stuck to the bottom of their shoe. They thought they were smarter than anyone else and didn't talk to you but proclamated. They were not smarter than anyone else and some were downright mean, sour, and vindictive. No one dared to run in election against them because if lost "go straight to hell".

Fortunately this all changed with the old guard passing. A new crop came in and with few exceptions the new crop is generally knowledgeable, speaks to you like you are a human being, and generally rule without prejudice and with an attitude that is reasonably conciliatory and while the decision may be against you, vanquished without being beat with the staff of justice. They may feel bad and left the house mad after wife call them what she perceived they were, they don't take it out on you. They don't embarrass you in front of others. These are a few exceptions we have one in Toombs County. She is not normal and very insecure. She could complementary by her emotional need to contact and connect everything before her court. She should not be judging anything.

Unfortunately, not all the dinosaurs are extinct. They make statements "it is our policy to do this, not it is justified under the circumstances, in fact, how can there be policies, each case is different and should be ruled on justiciable based on facts of each case, not on policy. These dinosaurs seemed to hate job and make you feel as if it is inconvenient for them to listen to you.

They make statements "next time you come to a gun fight don't bring a knife" "you'll be back (before the court) indicating you are no good" This does not show much judicial demeanor and go to a circuit where everyone dreads appearing before judges, there is something wrong with judges. The female judge in particular looks at you when you are addressing her with a smirk as if to say "how dare you bother me with this asinine drivel and you are an uneducated lout for even bringing this up and bothering me". Probably

hormonal.

BLUBBERING CITY

There is a stage where they give you the good news and the bad news, the bad news being you have a "rare type of cancer and if you don't take treatments you are going to be dead in months." That brings on what I like to refer to as the blubbering episode.

The blubbering episode is all of a sudden, every time you think about what has happened to you, every time you think about these people, your children, your grandchildren that you may never see again, you think about your office, your business all those lawyers that are going to be crying at your funeral (that's a joke) and you know what, it is a strange thing the one or two people that you know that live in your home town that wouldn't much care if you died and I mean that sincerely. I can assure you that among my colleagues for who I have great respect the question did come up among a few of the lawyers, not the old guys but a few of the younger ones. It looks like we are going to have the Solicitor's job open. Well unfortunately for them I have gotten over the blubbering and it looks like I am at least on my way to finishing this term in which they are going to be old lawyers by then.

The blubbering comes when you can't think of anything except your disease. I don't mean that you are thinking about the disease itself but you are thinking about all the ramifications of what is going to happen. One of my questions used to be when I was the macho man, who was never going to get sick, never going to die, was I used to have a saying, "I'm not really worried about dying, I am just wondering what is going to really happen to me." What I mean by "what's gonna happen to me" is the essence of me, not thinking about heaven or hell but I am thinking about something that is part of or maybe unique to me. I have since discovered, of course, there is not much unique in me or much uniqueness about the people I see on the street every day. I can definitely make the statement that everybody cares about dying. I used to use this ole joke about the guy who goes to the doctor, and I have told it a thousand times to a thousand people the same joke, and we all always get a laugh out of it. That is when I used to say I never go to the damn doctor there isn't nothing wrong with me. If you go to the doctor they will find something wrong with you and they will hurt you. I used to always go the doctor and I would come back and tell the doctor he said I only have 6 months to live and one of them would say don't say that but everybody else would laugh cause they knew what was coming next, but doctor, I can't pay my bill in 6 months and the doctor would say in that case I will give you 12 months to live. Now my secretary brought this home to me after I went to the doctor and he said you got months to live, she looked right at me and she said I sure hope you told him you couldn't pay the bill in 6 months. For the record, I couldn't think of anything funny at that point.

The blubbering stage begins when, of course this was going to be a big secret, and nobody in town was going to know about it. I was doing a pretty good job until I disappeared off the face of the earth and everybody said well, where is what's his name, the one that practices law he has an office up there somewhere around McDonald's, Flash Foods, or the Brice Cinema, what happened to him I haven't see him in two or three weeks. Oh, "he's sick", well what's wrong with him, "Well, we don't really know" but of course, by that time the word begins to get out and now everybody knows and then they went and put it on the radio about my leave of absence because I was taking chemo at hail-Mayo that pretty well destroyed the unknown of the man on his knees.

I am dictating this book and my wife comes out, now I have just finished two treatments today she says your medicine hasn't kick in yet has it? I said, no I haven't felt it yet. She says how do you feel and I said suicidal and she shook her head and went on in the room. Now G.O.D., I have just told my wife I was suicidal and she just sort of gave me a crazy look and goes on to bed. I am just curious do you think that is grounds for divorce. Please address that in your answer to this inquiry.

Blubbering is that feeling sorry for yourself that you go through and it takes about 10 days to get over it and then on occasion thereafter, particularly during treatment, you begin to blubber but it is usually just a passing moment and I meant that to be about like 5 or 10 minutes when you are talking to somebody, not necessarily somebody who you have an emotional attachment to but somebody that you particularly believe have a genuine concern for you, you blubber a bit.

Blubbering is that state you go through where you feel so sorry for yourself that you can't talk to anybody about your problem without blubbering. A lot of people call, a lot of people come to see you, you don't really want anybody coming to see you because if you blubber on the phone it is not as obvious although it is usually obvious but if they come to see you and tell you how concerned they are, you begin to blubber. It is just not something that you want to face during this blubbering period. It is not just friends, it's your children, your children's wives, your secretaries, it's everybody. About the first time you think you are over the blubbers you get sick and blubbers start all over again.. Basically, for some people the disease is just more or less like something you respond to but sometimes you have no symptoms and then again sometimes you do have symptoms but in my case G.O.D. I had very few symptoms after the operations but would still blubber. The blubbering is caused by that overwhelming knowledge that this is something that is not your friend, it will kill you without any conscience, with indifference, and every time you think of these things you wonder what did I ever do to deserve this, what caused this.

There are no answers to these questions; it is in the scheme of things that just happen. I doubt if any deity imposed this upon you and there appears to be some doubt whether some deity will unimpose this disease, this is what you realize when you blubber, once you are diagnosed you are a victim that rely on others to make you a non victim and sometimes they are successful and then sometimes they are not only successful but you don't receive the right treatment for your problem and many times what treatment, no matter what you receive the disease is still going to be the victor. This is what causes the blubbers because while you don't conscientiously think of this long list of reasons, it is there and you know it is there and you know it is true. Whatever you want to say is the strongest thing in the world, that's the truth, because no matter what you do you can't alter it.

The problem comes when you never call your friends back and all the concerned people but then you finally do call. The first thing you say is " I simply could not talk about this without blubbering but now I think I am over it and I want to talk to you and I want to tell you all about it". Of course, they are relieved because they don't want to listen to you blubber because they have not been there and they don't understand the blubbering. A few have been there. You finally go to see a good old friend, ya'll have shared a lot of secrets and a lot of things, you don't hold back much from one another and you look at your friend and say "well, hell I thought I was gonna bury you and now looks like you are gonna bury me" you want to be light about it but if you haven't waited long enough and then again, you may not can wait long enough, the blubbering is going to come and you are embarrassed about it but you didn't do anything to deserve this. I don't believe anybody does anything to deserve this disease.

Then it all begins to work out and sort of comes together and only on rare occasions you feel that "hot" feeling swelling up in you and your eyes begin to get a little red. This feeling gets rarer and rarer and the most amazing thing is, you get to believing and it may be true that you are going to make it. You immediately begin to hear all the stories like my cousin had it forty-eight years ago and she is still alive, etc, etc, etc.

Even if you do make it, there is always doubt when you go back for a check-up, am I making it or am I not making it? You may very well feel like a million bucks but you ain't making it. It is unimaginable the blubber if you go through months of treatment, you feel good, you look good, you're doing good and then you go back to that fifth check-up and they say we have some good news and some bad news. The bad news is its back, the good news we have laid out a whole new regimen for you and this time it is going to take care of it, talk about blubbering. Another thing that brings on the blubbering, is people hug you and say they are going to pray for you, you don't think about them personally, but you think if their praying was gonna help it would have happened way before this. You have mixed emotions about it, you would never say don't pray for me but you think to yourself, this is really a great guy or great girl and he or she is going to pray for you and it can't hurt anything and you hate that you don't think the prayer is going to help and that starts the blubbering all over again.

THIRTY FIVE IN A TWENTY FIVE
(35 in a 25)

My client walked in office, a mulatto looking guy, extremely well starched and neatly dressed cleaned shaven and coffered, and in a well-reasoned and educated clear voice told me he had been charged in this small biased town with driving 35 mph in a 25mph speed limit zone.

My liberal learnings immediately rose to the fore and realized was looking at prejudicial police brutality at its rawest. I was incensed and immediately began to plan to right this grievous wrong.

I girted my loins with the armor of righteous indignation and with shoulders held back marched to that den of injustice, intending to, with rapier like precision, cut this cancer of injustice from civilization.

I haughtily approached the officer knowing my countenance and reasoning would cover him into apologetic submission.

I explain my position philosophically peppered with legalese and was prepared to watch him fall to his knees in the face of my argument.

He looked at me I thought rather strangely and in a clear calm voice said, "your client was driving down the road backwards."

I felt my sphincter muscle tighten, my buttocks grab, my shoulders slump and face began to redden. My voice would not come but making a face of as much dignity as could muster and holding my head high, and wanting to become invisible, gargled and mumbled incoherently, and causally walked and walked and walked.

WHO HAS FAILED WHO IN THE I HAVE A DREAM

Martin Luther King was a visionary but probably did not have the practical vision to carry out the dream or even jump-start it. He would have needed the help of the honkies who have failed to do their part to make progress toward the dream, sorta like doing good works to get to heaven.

It's like the churches who consume most of its income on themselves, not on doing good work.

One black leader after the other speaks, "we have not made enough progress".

Whose fault is it? Maybe it is their fault when the black leaders allow a black prison population to soar to 70% of the total population. When our president speaks out against Zimmerman but doesn't utter a word about the homicidal black who shoots a white baby one year old and doesn't condemn the mother who hides the gun or the aunt who prepares him an alibi "he was eating breakfast at my house when it happen?"

The problem is blacks do not take responsibility for their actions or other black brothers actions. How about the three blacks killed a white boy because they needed a little excitement, where are the condemnations? It wasn't really the black boys fault after all they are black and because of their blacklist they are one of the brothers and its honky's fault. Black folks don't criticize because when the blame is laid on them, honky can no longer be blamed.

The republicans are right, for once in a blue moon, make the blacks take the blame, cut off their money, the blacks have made little progress and the money does not seem to help. They have as a whole not assimilated into American civilization. They insist on odd names, (so on job applications, it is immediately known what race person is without seeing that person) and cannibal hair. If that is what MLK's dream is, so be it, but don't blame honky for failure of any progress. Keep shooting one another but don't be surprised when prison population continues to soar and honky becomes more and more down on you and pulls back on any help on Dream because primarily no black wants to stand up and say its my fault. Responsibility must be taken before there can be any progress on the dream.

THE OPPOSABLE THUMB

There are many strange things and strange behaviors that come into contact in our lives.

I had a friend, very astute professional, who began with alcohol, marijuana, and then coke and possible other "prescriptions". Unbeknownst to me he also was addicted to women and apparently enjoyed a little whoopee in the hay. He eventually was married three times and divorced two times. The first harbinger of his leanings became apparent when myself, my friend and a female friend decided the tension in our lives required we relax in a local bar. It was about four in the afternoon.

We arrived in separate cars at the pub and began to drink. It was a little round table and our seating arrangement was the female in the middle with us on the either side. As we drink, I decided to cop a feel and sneakingly ran my hand under the table to see what treasure might be there. Instead of the smooth texture of a thigh felt this boney hand. My friend had arrived at the station before me.

We became rather intoxicated and decided it was time to go back to paradise with our wives. I was in a quandary of an explanation why we were out so late drinking and more importantly, cross-examination might be intense.

I suggested to my friend he write a note to my wife that we had been researching a perplexing legal question and I would write a note to his wife stating the same.

We wrote the notes in the bar and journeyed outside to cars. By that time, I had a premonition those notes would be suspect to our wives. I threw mine in the trashcan. He carried his home and was divorced three months later.

Time passed and he remarried and we, three lawyers, gave him a party at my house. It was a gay occasion and my children particularly thought my friend was a great guy, sort of a character, in a good sense. I will never forget he wore a solid white outfit and looked rather dapper in a juke joint sort of way. When you come out the back door of the house, you must take an immediate right to go down steps, which the porch is about three feet off ground. My friend being somewhat loose walked straight to back of porch and fell. My kids had been watching him with both eyes and they described fall to be as if his feet did not hit ground but he did a porpoise loop, stomach first, and came up immediately on his feet and while kids admired the gymnastics they were enthralled and amazed that there was not a grass or dirt stain on his white suit. It was as if he never touched the ground but looped about three inches from grass, sort of an anti gravity trick, and stood up unscathed. Probably one of the modern miracles of our time.

My family always went to the beach for month of July and friend always went with us for about a week and by that time had two beautiful little girls and they would go to beach. As we left for beach, my wife commented we would probably kill those girls. She was just kidding.

We departed and stopped at every outdoor bar on the way finally stopping at a biker's club and went in and ordered. The biker's loved the girls and we had a great time. My friend said the meal that night at beach was on him, I protested, but he stated he was saving the money and had put in his bra for safekeeping. He was joking. I don't think he had on a bra.

It took about three hours at beach before he would, under influence of the grape, proclaimed as soon as he returned home he was selling his office and moving his practice to the beach in Florida.

He would occasionally get off a good one, once, I commented to him this girl passing by sexed me up and he replied road kill sexed me up. I think he meant it didn't take much to sex me up.

As time went by it appeared he was having trouble in his present marriage caused by the thigh upon which he had his boney hand on that faithful night of the notes to the wives, "we were working".

Gossip had it the thigh upon which the boney hand was resting was pregnant by the boney-handed villain and a child had been produced and friend was paying child support. I counseled for a DNA test but he declined to follow that advice and stated he may do so in the future.

The love child had reached the age of about four and had the occasion to play with him and noticed his hands and in particular his thumbs, which I immediately recognized as being identical to my friends thumbs which had certain unusual characteristic. There was little doubt of who was the father of the child and so informed my friend and told him to forget DNA test.

In the annals of paternity this is probably the first case opposable thumbs have proved fatherhood. It's a long way to Tipperary, it's long way to go, it's a long way to Tipperary, to the sweetest girl I know.

DON'T CARE HOW LONG WE STAY

I remember trying a case, child molestation, a rather clean molestation case, no penetration or touching but inappropriate behavior. We were trying the case because the inappropriate behavior seemed extremely questionable. The child was the stepchild of the defendant husband and child of the wife from a previous skirmish.

The wife had filed for a divorce wanting the parties' home, which the husband had remodeled through his own efforts and money. He worked two jobs. She was never employed during the marriage.

He came across as a good old boy, she rather witchery. My conclusion was she wanted to get rid of him and keep the house and what better way than "he molested my child". A jury would certainly be sympathetic to this plight.

It took about two days to try case.

The jury went out and surprisingly after two hours came back and foremen stated they were not going to reach a verdict. The judge ran hot and lambasted the jury, saying that after two days of trial for only trying to reach a verdict for two hours and then stating were not going to reach a verdict. The judge rather hotly went on to say they would stay there through Saturday (it was Wednesday afternoon)" if need be.

I noticed there was one particular juror twisting and turning in her seat, face flushed, appearing extremely uncomfortable. I surmised then she was the hold out for "not guilty" the other eleven wanting to convict. I suspected some knowledge she had outside of what was presented in court.

On Thursday morning, the jury came back in and announced to judge "we don't care if we stay here through the next two Saturdays, (another week and one-half) we are not going to reach a verdict. I looked at who I thought was the hold out juror and she seemed calm but in my heart knew she was the hold out. She was a schoolteacher. Judge threw in the towel and declared a mistrial and jury went home.

The District Attorney Altman (DA) feeling that close to "victory" decided to retry.

We picked another jury, I ran out of strikes and took jurors would normally have excused. I ended up with several schoolteachers, not good, and several prominent busy men, not good. I felt my client was headed down the river, which disturbed me because, did not feel was guilty. The schoolteachers were also women, really not good. In those days, I would know literally everyone on the jury and had a sinking feeling this time around.

Shockingly the jury found not guilty after not too long deliberating.

The foreman was one of the prominent business men in Toombs County. I discovered later he had served on a murder trial many years before in which the girl friend had killed her lover. The town was shocked when she was found not guilty and I knew then I did not have a good insightful understanding of my foreman.

I knew in my heart that on the first trial the juror who held out was influenced by others who hated the mother of the child or truly felt defendant did not do what was alleged. I think they did not like the mother.

DEATH

It is against human nature to believe that when you die there is absolutely nothing else, not one drop of a soul, not one molecule left to go and be something else. It is hard to say but it simply means that whatever or how we existed is gone. Nothing is left. The one caveat to that is, probably there is nothing unique in us that is not in plentiful supply around. So since we have no uniqueness then nothing has been destroyed. Because what we possessed, is everywhere. Maybe in abundance and maybe better uniqueness than our uniqueness.

HE BORROWED PAPER

I remember being in the sixth grade and a boy sat behind me who everyday borrowed paper to write on. A pack of paper cost five cents and there were only sixteen sheets in a pack. He never had any paper.

Compared to today's poor and the number of people who are poor, everyone was poor at that time. For example in those days, maybe one or two students drove an automobile to school. These days you are lucky to be able to find a parking place at school and it seems there are more than two cars in every family.

Those days many families did not even own one car and always walked everywhere they went, if they ever went anywhere. I remember my family borrowing a car to go to a funeral.

When the families went to town on Saturday to buy groceries and after bagging, the store had a place to leave groceries and so after getting transportation you would come by and pickup but often carried purchases home in their arms.

I do not recall any one losing their purchases although many families had groceries stacked in the same place, would leave there for several hours from morning to afternoon, and then would pick up.

Gas for cars was nineteen cents per gallon.

I complained to borrower when kept asking for paper. One morning he walked in and gave me a whole pack of paper, sixteen sheets, a whole nickel's worth.

I felt guilty about taking the paper and told him to just give me a few sheets, but he insisted take the whole pack.

Children do things that in their mind mean nothing but deep down in the depths of their being there's a spark of something good God puts in even children, they don't know it but act on feelings which instinctively make them feel good.

They will forget it soon enough, but there's a little mark there that says well done and remains, not consciously, but a little thing that remains forever.

SALTAVICH

When I first moved back to Vidalia after failing in every enterprise which dreamed of would make me rich. One of the things that struck me was all my friends that grew up with were busy doing their thing and it was not quite like a standing ovation, welcome home.

I immediately met a new friend W.L. Salter who was a freshly anointed "attorney", he thought, little did he know, that all the attorneys are in Atlanta, the lawyers are in Vidalia or Tarrytown, wherever.

He opened an office across the street from my booming real estate business "we did not take in a copper" first six months open and W.L. was not exactly booming in his newly "salved" attorney practice across the street near post office.

We didn't have a lot to do so we spent a lot of time talking. In fact, when we finally got busy, we knew more about each other than we knew about ourselves. We talked about the philosophy of Socrates, Plato, and women.

One of our real social endeavors was to walk about 50 feet to Allmond's service station and get a coke. The problem was I did not have a quarter for a coke so would decline and W.L. finally, by some magic, gleamed I did not have the funds to buy a lowly coke and he would often treat me. W.L. seemed to always have money even though I know he must have thrown away millions on hair brain schemes outlined to him by his clients. His wife, Betty, was often put out about his schemes, which involved spending money.

He was a real friend and talked to me into going to law school. When we see him in heaven am going to have to talk to him about that.

THE PHALLIC TRAVELS

If you are a male or a female for that matter, you immediately notice it. When a little boy you rub it, look at it and are amazed at how satisfying to rub. Other than pee-peeing, it's a mystery why it's so much fun. Even growing up there is a mystery or an instinct about and what's it for but something in the back of your mind gleams pleasure and a good feeling.

Even at 2 or 3 years there is a wonderment why girls don't have one but you enjoy looking at where it ought to be. Oh, father can I leave my post now, the flames are getting higher. You show me yours and I'll show you mine, whatever yours and mine are. I remember showing mine and a mosquito had bitten the end and there was a red bulb there and she laughed, little did I know that was a harbinger of many laughs to come after that.

Little do we know but it was the answer to the population burst, couple with other organs, and an answer to many of the world problems. The idea came to me from the old custom of the Japanese of binding a young girls feet making them things of beauty.

There would have to be some controlled experimentation such as how far can healthy sperm travel. From the lips of the vagina over the little lip hill down the hill into the pleasure canal making its way to bingo pregnancy place, assuming there was no pull out, at the magic moment and the little sperms were clamoring for the opportunity to do their duty, sort of like a kamikaze pilot.

If it is determined, the little sperms could not climb the hill and make their way down the magic canal the population crisis is solved. We must first propagandize that a little phallic is a thing of beauty to be admired by all. In this misinformed society, huge is good, disdained by little ones who philosophize that it is not the size of the rapier but the skill by which it is used. Some have never believed that, not being one of the little ones. To make it work is bind the phallus, like feet, of Japanese girl, small feet are to be admired, it follows a small phallus is to be admired and if can't eject with force the little sperm can't make target, no pregnancy.

THEY DON'T GET IT

I snickered when several black preachers called a press conference in Savannah with God's help were calling for days of no violence, killings.

They pretend and maybe actually thought with God's help the black violent criminals would really be convinced and their primitive urges would be persuaded by people of their own race calling on them to do right. There was a killing within twenty-four hours, black on black. What they should have said we are bringing the black community together and ferreting out these primitive killers from our mist. Black should stop letting whites punish blacks for killing other blacks and blacks should begin their own punishment. The pro-football player who would not stand for the Banner, how ignorant, he is blaming white race, when he should be looking inward. He could stay on his knee all week for the blacks who killed more than 40 blacks in 2016 in Savannah alone. He has the disease, which is the trend that runs, blame anyone but us blacks.

The black chief can hire one million officers, which will have little influence on the problem. He must cast the blame on those whose fault it is, the black community, and when he points to the black community, and when he points to the black community, it's your fault and the problem must be solved from within and want be solved until focus is on us. It can be done one-step-at-a-time but the black community must take the first step and realize it's a black problem and stop blaming the honkies.

SOMETHING LEFT

I truly believe as you get older, something in your body changes...that your mind doesn't go but something in your body changes that makes you want to quit using your mind. You don't want the agony of thinking real hard. I also believe that you quit working your body, you quit messing with it, although there are certain things you can't change and it in turn... it is not your body that gives you out it is your will to make your body stay in good shape that gives out. The big question is ....what is it that changes in your body? It must be a chemical imbalance that makes you change, if we could correct that chemical imbalance then we could sustain our lives much longer, mentally and physically.

I don't think that it is a chemical imbalance, I think it is simply a point where we have reached full capacity and have in effect, in our minds at least, believe we have seen everything at least one time before. Having seen it before, boredom sets in which in effect leads to a slow down of the mind, a slowdown of the desire which is a slowdown of the mind, a slowdown of the physique, all because we have already run that extra mile, we have already lifted those extra weights, we have done all the things to keep in shape but we are bored with doing that.

We have read the books, at least all we had time for, we have seen all the movies, we have talked to everybody we could possibly ever want to and we have heard about almost every view in the whole world. What else is there we really want to do. Most of us will notice, as we get older, we don't want to have these conversations with people anymore. It is not because we don't find them interesting or their view may not be good, it is just that we simply are just not interested anymore.

Have you ever noticed how when people are together and there is an older person in the room, particularly a family older person, the conversation goes around them. They don't have much to say, even when you make an effort to bring them into the conversation, it simply doesn't work. It doesn't work to bring them into the conversation because they are not really interested in what we are saying, they don't have any new opinion because they know someone else has already voiced that opinion three times so therefore, they sit in silence.

There is one thing left to salve the wound of old age a child. There is nothing more comforting or that arouses your emotions more than when someone picks up a small child, holds them in their arms and walks with them by holding them gently at the tops of their legs underneath their buttocks or rump. The child knows that someone cares for them and is looking after them and is going to take them somewhere they will be safe. This act is usually done unselfishly, anything that shows an intrinsic shining through of God in a person is when you see them take a child gently in their arms, hold them and walk with them. The child may put their arms around the back of the neck of the person.

Look at that child with his arm around the back of the neck of the person who is carrying them, you can see into the eyes of the person they will do anything to protect the child and when you look into the eyes of the child you know they feel protected and comforted.

A CHANGE OF SPIRIT

We moved through life and as we do there are certain goals we hope to achieve and it is not a specific goal, like becoming President of the United States but a general feeling to have a satisfying and in your mind successful life. We want to do things such as go to work every day, make a decent living, and feel as if we are important in the sense we are doing the right thing, and we do this constantly and this gives us a sense of well-being, in other words, we're happy. But our little bumps, holes in the road of our life are temporary things but overcome them and still travel forward with a certain sense that all is relatively well and we are moving forward in our life and are working toward certain goals. Most of the times those goals are not definitive, they are just a sense that we have and are going forward. I know we begin these feelings, ambitions, at a very young age and always feel as if we are moving forward, and have a relative sense of importance in this world and while we may fail the geometry test it is not something that changes our movement forward.

We do this for years, and years, and years, and one thing is eventually going to happen, that is, we get old and realize that many of our feelings we are moving forward with will no longer have any real meaning, in other words, instead of having a feeling of importance we come to the realization, we are not as important as we thought we were. However, we rationalize this and instead of moving forward with certain goals in mind or a certain feeling we are accomplishing goals, we just move forward but this still does not make us unhappy. It is a process in which inside of most of us there have been preparations for such time, we weather it very well, we do very well, life simply moves forward, and we are relatively happy.

What can happen in our lives, and it happens to some of us but not all of us, is a shadowing event that changes our relatively sense of importance and well-being and we feel as if all of a sudden we cannot move forward. Our muscles have no life and our thoughts have absolutely no meaning. The tragedy of all this is, often, we cannot overcome it. It may happen to us at thirty-five years of age when it really should have happened to us at seventy years of age. Even at seventy it is not the same because we realize because we are seventy things have changed our lives. Whereby at age thirty-five we cannot put these changes in our mind and cannot realize that this this has not been a normal movement through life but something abruptly has killed the feeling of any possible ambition and well-being we might have of ourselves. Often these events are not our fault but we cannot overcome it, we are listless and nothing seems important any longer. It often takes years to overcome this listless feeling and every time we think of this event we have a dread warm feeling in our body. Food has no meaning, hugs, kisses, compliments; criticisms have no meaning in our lives. Whereas, before we wanted to make a difference, now, it makes no difference.

What can some of these events possibly be? The most common event that can cause this is the loss of a child and particularly an only child. The child occupied a part of our movement through life, was part of that movement, and was one of the things, which pushed us on. The child looked up to us and made us feel important although we might not have been worth fifty cents. We doted on that feeling. It made us get up in the morning, it encouraged us to get up in the morning and go to work, get the child off to school, pick the child up, buy the child gifts, play with the child, take them to work with us, take them to church on Sunday, take him to the movies, take him to the fair. He was a part of our life and he gave us the resolve to go forward and a reason to enjoy life. Once the child is no longer there, there is no enjoyment. We say that the strong can overcome this and move forward. It may not be the strong at all perhaps the weak are the ones that can overcome and move forward. Our whole outlook toward life has changed. We are in a vacuum. Our mind cannot think, our muscles feel like lead, and we are listless. No matter how strong, how weak we are we eventually do make some sort of adjustment, but it is never out of our lives.

Eventually occasions arise where we have a momentary forgetfulness on this horrible event but laying down at night and going to sleep we always remember, we wake up early, and for a second or two after we wake up we can't remember but then it is back in our mind again.

The question arises why would God do this? It is certainly not news the tired and worn out "God does what's best for us", "God looks after us", "it is not for us to understand." Many would say "God is with us all the time and is carrying us through this", Well maybe so, maybe not, but one thing is for sure most never get a word from God, all is well which settles our mind, body, and spirit. Probably not going to happen. No one is going to help us in some mysterious way we can't figure out. If we can't figure it out it certainly can't help us very much.

So what are we to do? Perhaps God has given us that inalienable spirit that is to carry us through these events. We all have to believe what we believe. If we have this spirit or part of God in us perhaps, we can get through this and change but it will never leave us.

Some are willing to die and some do take that route but most do not. We go on with our life after a while, perhaps someone comes into our life that is going to change us, and maybe that is part of the gift God gave us. He gave us the capacity to adjust, there is no question we have the capacity to adjust, and we go on and on but probably the last thought we have before our life ends, is of that terrible event that took place many, many years before.

FINALLY LEGAL

In the 40's and before everyone drove, many did not have driver's license. After a bicycle, driving a motor vehicle was an assent into heaven, the epitome of life a pleasure beyond description, similar to when at 16 years of age, fantasizing about the girl in your high school that awakens your imagination when she moves and sometimes get to see flesh about three inches above the ankle and wildly fantasize into outer space when glimpse a knee.

I remember when the magic day came, reached sixteen and eligible for a driver's license. There were no books to study for a written and can't remember how knew answers to test questions. Probably from that bunch that hung out together. They knew everything.

My father owned a nondescript Pickup truck that can best be described as minimum transportation. But we were proud.

The happy day arrived and daddy took me in truck to Reidsville State Prison, where State Patrol Office was located. You had to take a driving test and a written exam.

The trooper that "greeted" us was 17 feet tall, his boots were at least three feet up his legs, and he looked down scornfully on me. I was scared.

The test was given, graciously described as secured, everyone set at tables, across from one another by each other, and was extremely easy to see other's papers. In those days, cheating was a sin and the cheater was looked down upon. Not so in the twentieth century, to get by now is a badge of accomplishment and others admire your cunning.

On this particular day, there were about twelve taking the written test and there was a very young looking kid whose Grandfather had brought to get license. He looked about "ten" years old. Everyone was in room together, persons taking the test, parents who had brought those purportedly ready to drive into the world, and troopers. As we began the test, pencil and paper, the "ten" year old asked, out loud his grandfather, a question about something on the test. Trooper said can't do that. He did it again, admonish by trooper again, did it again, and trooper picked up his paper. He left with grandfather, a wronged sour hurt look on his face.

All of the sudden all the troopers jumped up and rushed outside. As it turned out the "ten" year old got under the driver's seat of grandfather's car and backed into a State Patrol vehicle.

I don't know exactly what happened there after.

I finished my test and when finished carried up to trooper at a desk and he graded it while you stood there and would comment to you. One of the questions was "how far away from approaching car should dim lights? I had checked 300 feet but right answer is 500 feet, trooper grader said "close enough" and gave me credit, how the world has changed.

I passed and trooper took me outside to drive, asked, "does this thing have good brakes", I dutifully said yes sir. You sired grownups in those days and in particularly people in a position of authority.

I passed and got driver's license.

Don't know what happened to the "ten" year old.

WHAT

September 9, 1999

There is no question civilization is careening to a fiery violent end, a religion shall play a big part. It there is a God he has created a humanoid, that is innate and with unlimited capacity for violence and cruelty. The other capacity the human race has is a mind bent that absolutely refuses to see the right or wrong of anything. This varies with different people. If it doesn't suit their particular perspective or vision or version of what is right or wrong they are going to seek revenge or do whatever violence is necessary to have their vision or their version of the event to become what it is.

This is because of murder, crime, violence against nations, against churches and the mayhem that follows. It is unbelievable that God has created a race of people, said all life is sacred, and created the kind of crap we have on this earth who destroys life without any compunction. If there is a God it is time he took a hand in these events.

Now the Christians have rationalized this into a concept that the devil causes bad and God takes credit for all the good. This of course is a rationalization that would justify this concept. These very Christians are the ones that will do whatever is necessary to have their version or their vision of what life should be and put in place. God hasn't given them the capacity to see that what they believe may be wrong.

Many Christians believe or purport to believe.

One of the characteristics of getting old is you can only talk about the past. There is no future. You are not building a new house or you are not buying another car, you are not trying to get a promotion, you are not looking for a new job, you are looking for some sort of steady income, not big, but enough that you can live fairly comfortably on knowing that all you're ever going to get might even be in danger.

When you are around all your friends you don't talk about the future, you talk about all the things you've done in the past and what you might do that day but as far as talking about doing anything that is a long range project, you don't do that. You may talk about planting a few plants in the year or adding a little on to your house or maybe even getting your car worked on that day, what you read in the paper, a little politics, there is nothing substantial you talk about that you are going to do in the future because you literally have no future.

When your grandchildren are little and they want to be around you and play with you and do things with you but as they get older they then have their own friends and they don't really have much in common with you after that. They want you to go to the ballgame and see them play and see them play the piano and do little things but after a while their interest changes completely and it gets down to seeing you maybe on your birthday, if their mother can make them go or maybe getting the mower at Christmas. Then when you really get old and really get feeble, you sit at the table with everybody talking but nobody says anything to you and there is nothing for you to say because what they are talking about has no relevance to you. You are marked in time. And while everybody still loves you and wants to look after you and help you there is no common thread there anymore.

The plus side of all this is if you lived a relatively decent life and you've got a little bit of money to live off of and your kids are still around and they still help you and look after you and they still love you, you can be satisfied with this arrangement. The fact is you can do things that you never had time to do before although they're not very substantive things in the sense that you are not working on big projects, maybe you are just learning some things, you read a lot in the paper and you watch a little tv and you do have time to do things that you may want to do.

You can go and have your hair done but you are limited if you are a man you probably only have two or three. You get your hair cut because you want to be around people not because you much care about your hair or there is much there to cut. Fact is are probably more concerned about that lesion, skin cancer, that is come on your skin because as you get old all the diseases get you and mess with you.

I had a nephew killed in a car accident, a couple months past. It must have been around June or July 1998 maybe later.

He was a different kind of a kid in the sense that he was highly intelligent and you could not just sit down and have a casual conversation about things because he had such a wealth of knowledge he told you more than you ever wanted to know. He did have a sense of humor though and he was a hard working guy.

The tragedy was devastating to his parents who were in their early 60's . Not much chance of another child and it was devastating to them. Their life didn't revolve around him but it was a big part of it. It would be nice to think that in some euphoric place they will all meet again.

There is not much to support the theory that will ever happen. If you are a Christian, a true believing Christian, then you of course believe this but it is extremely difficult to really believe the concept that a person whose body functions have ceased and there is no life there that he will ever have life again. A tragedy of epic proportions, God gave us the capacity to love, the capacity to hate, the capacity to murder and he actually gave us the capacity to go on with our lives after these tragedies. It would be hard to imagine a life where we did not become highly attached to other people although it is possible and it would have saved many, many hours of grief but if we take away the grief, we would have to take away the truly wonderful emotion of love. In other words, if we took away all of that, we wouldn't recognize ourselves or others. We would be zombies.

I went to a funeral the other day where the gentleman was 87 years old. Surprising there were many younger people in their 70's who knew him very well and there is something about when you get old people are attracted to you in the sense that they remember all about you and they want to speak to you and they want to see how you are doing. Maybe they see themselves as being your age and they want to somehow compensate by talking or telling you how glad they are to see you. It is wonderful though to be with someone that age and everyone flocks to see him, everyone wants to hold his hand or pat him on the back or talk with him. That is a mystery why people feel that way. I think it has something to do with a common bond and, that is, most of their lives are over, and they somehow want to compensate by drawing closer.

The problem is when you get so old, you have a drink at the bar with a friend they don't want to take you home, they will look at a 30 year old gal who is walking by with the tight blue-jeans even though you would probably be a much better partner they don't think of you in terms of that, they want the youth. We all want the youth.

It is really quite odd because the older person maybe much better but that is the way God made us, it is his problem not ours and it is his fault not ours.

Made in the USA
Columbia, SC
12 June 2021